2.50

JOHN CREASEY'S
CRIME COLLECTION
1990

JOHN CREASEY'S CRIME COLLECTION 1990

An Anthology by members of the Crime Writers' Association

edited by

HERBERT HARRIS

LONDON
VICTOR GOLLANCZ LTD
1990

First published in Great Britain 1990
by Victor Gollancz Ltd,
14 Henrietta Street, London WC2E 8QJ

The right of Judy Chard, Basil Copper, Antonia Fraser, Michael Gilbert,
Peter Godfrey, Glyn Hardwicke, Herbert Harris, H. R. F. Keating, Peter
Lovesey, Jean McConnell, Mike Ripley, George Sims, Ian Stuart, Julian
Symons, Tony Wilmot and Margaret Yorke to be identified as contribu-
tors to this work has been asserted by them in accordance with the
Copyright Designs and Patents Act 1988

British Library Cataloguing in Publication Data
John Creasey's crime collection 1990
    Crime short stories in English 1945–
    Anthologies
    I. Creasey, John, *1908–1973*   II. Harris,
    Herbert, *1911–*

ISBN 0–575–04828–X

Typeset at The Spartan Press Ltd,
Lymington, Hants
Printed in Great Britain by St Edmundsbury Press Ltd,
Bury St Edmunds, Suffolk

CONTENTS

ACKNOWLEDGMENTS

Acknowledgments are due to *Verdict of 13* (Faber & Faber) for "Waiting for Mr McGregor" by Julian Symons; *Butchers and Other Stories of Crime* (Macmillan) for "Private Gorman's Luck" by Peter Lovesey; *Mrs Craggs — Crimes Cleaned Up* (Buchan & Enright) for "A Dangerous Thing, Mrs Craggs" by H.R.F. Keating; *Ellery Queen's Mystery Magazine* for "Anniversary" by Margaret Yorke, "Dicker McLeish's Girl" by Ian Stuart, and "The Stairs of Sand" by Peter Godfrey; *Petrella at Q* (Hodder & Stoughton) for "The Last Tenant" by Michael Gilbert; *International Story Teller* for "Destroying Angel" by Judy Chard; *Voices of Doom* (Robert Hale) for "The Madonna of the Four-Ale Bar" by Basil Copper; *Weekend* for "Life Sentence" by Tony Wilmot; *Bella* for "Last Post" by Jean McConnell; *Brewer's Guardian* for "Gold Sword" by Mike Ripley; and *Opera Now* for "Out for the Countess" by Antonia Fraser. Original stories in this collection are "The Elixir" by Glyn Hardwicke, "Two of a Kind" by Herbert Harris, and "The Rules of the Game" by George Sims.

INTRODUCTION

In the twenty-four collections of short stories which I have edited for the Crime Writers' Association, I have often, in my Introductions, stressed the value of such anthologies in preserving the miniature art of fiction.

I am sure that publishers seldom, if ever, make fortunes from short story collections, but the few who continue to bring them out must derive much satisfaction from the perpetuation of an art form evolved from the ancient parables and fables common to all mankind.

The CWA's sister organisation in the USA, Mystery Writers of America, honours the short story by presenting annual awards called "Edgars", after Edgar Allan Poe, regarded by many as the father of the modern short story. The CWA, which presents annual "Daggers", has not as yet any "Arthurs" in honour of Conan Doyle; but no matter, we do have some splendid story collections and still a few publishers virtuous enough to publish them.

As a boy I feasted greedily on The Masterpiece Library of Short Stories, edited by J. A. Hammerton, which ran to twenty volumes. I cannot claim to have matched the brilliance of the nineteenth-century masters in the stories selected for my own twenty-four volumes, but I think the discerning reader will have found some "near greats" in past CWA collections, and will find some more of the same quality in this one.

HERBERT HARRIS

WAITING FOR MR McGREGOR

Julian Symons

PRELUDE

Even in these egalitarian English days nannies are still to be seen in Kensington Gardens, pushing ahead of them the four-wheeled vehicles that house the children of the rich. On a windy day in April a dozen perambulators were moving slowly in the direction of the Round Pond, most of them in pairs. The nannies all wore uniforms. Their charges were visible only as well-wrapped bundles, some of them waving gloved fists into the air.

The parade was watched by more people than usual. A blond young man sat on a bench reading a newspaper. A pretty girl at the other end of the bench looked idly into vacancy. A rough-looking character pushed a broom along a path in a desultory way. The next bench held a man in black jacket, striped trousers and bowler hat reading the *Financial Times*, a man of non-descript appearance with his mouth slightly open and a tramplike figure who was feeding pigeons with crumbs from a paper bag. Twenty yards away, another young man leaned against a lamppost.

A pram with a crest on its side approached the bench where the blond young man sat. The nanny wore a neat cap and a blue-striped uniform. Her baby could be seen moving about and a wail came from it, but its face was hidden by the pram hood. The pram approached the bench where the man in the black jacket sat.

The blond young man dropped his newspaper. The group moved into action. The young man and the girl, the three people at the next bench, the man beside the lamppost and the man pushing the broom took from their pockets masks which they fitted over their faces. The masks were of animals. The blond young man was a rabbit, the girl a pig, the others a squirrel, a rat, another pig, a cat and a frog.

The masks were fitted in a moment, and the animal seven converged upon the pram with the crest on its side. Half a dozen people nearby stood and gaped, and so did other nannies. Were they all rehearsing a scene for a film, with cameras hidden in the bushes? In any case, English reticence forbade interference, and they merely watched or turned away their heads. The nanny beside the pram uttered a well-bred muted scream and fled. The child in the pram cried lustily.

The blond young man was the first beside the pram, with the girl just after him. He pushed down the hood, pulled back the covers and recoiled at what he saw. The roaring baby in the pram was of the right age and looked of the right sex. There was just one thing wrong about the baby. It was coal black.

The young man looked at the baby disbelievingly for a moment, then shouted at the rest of them: "It's a plant. Get away, fast."

The words came distorted through the mask, but their sense was clear enough, and they followed accepted procedure, scattering in three directions and tearing off the masks as they went. Pickup cars were waiting for them at different spots in the Bayswater Road, and they reached them without misadventure except for the tramp, who found himself confronted by an elderly man brandishing an umbrella.

"I saw what you were doing, sir. You were frightening that poor—"

The tramp swung a loaded cosh against the side of his head. The elderly man collapsed.

The baby went on roaring. The nanny came back to him. When he saw her he stopped roaring and began to chuckle.

Somebody blew a police whistle, much too late. The cars all got away without trouble.

"What happened?" asked the driver of the car containing the blond young man and the pretty girl.

"It was a plant," he said angrily. "A bloody plant."

TRIAL AND VERDICT

Hilary Engels Mannering liked to say that his life had been ordered by his name. With a name like Hilary Mannering, how could one fail to be deeply aesthetic in nature? (How the syllables positively flowed off the tongue!) And Engels, the name insisted on by his mother because she had been reading Engels's account of conditions among the Manchester poor a day or two before his birth — if one was named Engels, wasn't one almost in duty bound to have revolutionary feelings? Others attributed the pattern of Hilary's adult life to his closeness to his mother and alienation from his father. Others said that an only child of such parents was bound to be odd. Others still talked about Charlie Ramsden.

Johnny Mannering, Hilary's father, was a cheerful extrovert, a wine merchant who played tennis well enough to get through the preliminary rounds at Wimbledon more than once, had a broken nose and a broken collarbone to show for his courage at rugby, and when rugby and tennis days were over became a scratch golfer. To say that Johnny was disappointed in his son would be an understatement. He tried to teach the boy how to hold a cricket bat, gave Hilary a tennis racquet for his tenth birthday and patted the ball over the net to him endlessly. Endlessly and uselessly. "What I can't stand is that he doesn't even try," Johnny said to his wife, Melissa. "When the ball hit him on the leg today — a tennis ball, mind you — he started snivelling. He's what you've made him, a snivelling little milksop."

Melissa took no notice of such remarks, and indeed hardly seemed to hear them. She had a kind of statuesque blank beauty which concealed a deep dissatisfaction with the comfortable life that moved between a manor house in Sussex and a large apartment in Kensington. She should have been — what should she have been? A rash romantic poet, a heroine of some lost revolution, an explorer in Africa, anything but what she was, the wife of a wealthy sporting English wine merchant. She gave to Hilary many moments of passionate affection to which he passionately responded, and days or even months of neglect.

In the nursery years which many psychologists think the most important of our lives, Hilary was cared for by big-bosomed Anna, who washed and bathed him, wiped his bottom when he was dirty, and read to him endlessly the stories of Beatrix Potter. Peter Rabbit, Squirrel Nutkin and Samuel Whiskers, Pigling Bland and Jeremy Fisher, became figures more real to the small boy than his own parents. And brooding over all these nursery characters, rather as Hilary's father brooded with angry discontent over his unsatisfactory household, was the farmer Mr McGregor, who had put Peter Rabbit's father into a pie, and whose great foot could be seen in one illustration about to come down on Peter. Anna read and Hilary shivered, finding in the figure of the farmer an image of his own frightening father.

Childhood does not last forever, but there are those who cling to childish things rather than putting them away. Hilary went up to Oxford — which to Johnny Mannering was still the only possible university — in the early Sixties, just before the days of the Beatles and permissiveness. There he displayed the collected works of Beatrix Potter on his shelves beside books more fashionable for an undergraduate. "But, my dear, these are the existential masterpieces of the century," he said in his pleasant, although thin and slightly fluting, voice. "The passions, the deceits, the *poignancy* of it all; really, Proust and Joyce are nothing to it." Beatrix Potter gave him the only celebrity he achieved at Oxford. He joined two or three radical groups and left them within a few weeks, did a little acting but could not remember his lines, had three poems published in a small magazine.

He had just one friend, a broad-shouldered, blond, puzzled-looking rugger blue named Charlie Ramsden, who had been at Hilary's public school, and had always regarded him as a genius. This view was not changed when Hilary took as poor a degree as his own, something they both attributed to the malice of the examiners. Hilary, on his side, treated Charlie with the affectionate superiority one might give to a favourite dog. "You must meet Charlie," he would say to new acquaintances. "He's terribly good at *rugby football*." Charlie would smile ruefully, rub his nose and say, "'Fraid I am." They were really, as the acquaintances remarked with astonishment, almost inseparable. Not long after he came down, Hilary surprised his friends, not to mention his parents, by marrying a girl he had met in his last year at Oxford. Joyce was the daughter of an old and enormously rich family, and the wedding got a good deal of attention from gossip writers. Charlie Ramsden was best man.

The marriage was six months old when Johnny Mannering, driving home with Melissa after a party, skidded on an icy road and went over the central barrier into the lane of oncoming traffic, where his car was hit head on by a lorry. Both Johnny and Melissa were killed immediately. At the age of twenty-five Hilary found himself the distinctly rich owner of the family business. Within another six months his marriage had ended. Hilary never told anybody what was in the note that Joyce left upon the drawing room mantelpiece of their house in Belgravia, beyond saying that she had done the boringly conventional thing as usual. There was no doubt, however, that she had gone away with a man, and his identity did cause surprise. The man was Charlie Ramsden.

Hilary divorced Joyce, she married Charlie, and they settled in South Africa, where he became a farmer. Those closest to Hilary (but nobody was very close to him) said that he recovered from the loss of Joyce, but that he never forgave Charlie Ramsden. He never mentioned either of them again. In the years that followed, he gathered the biggest collection of Beatrix Potter manuscripts, first editions and association copies in the world, put up money for a radical magazine, with which he became bored after a couple of issues, and for two plays, both of which were flops. He travelled abroad a good deal, sometimes in the company of young actors who appeared in the plays. In Amsterdam, on one of these trips, he met Klaus Dongen.

Klaus was half Dutch, half German, a revolutionary terrorist who believed that destruction of all existing national states must precede the advent of a free society. His group, the NLG or Netherlands Liberation Group, claimed credit for half-a-dozen assassinations, including one of a prominent Dutch politician, for a bomb that blew up in a crowded restaurant, and another in a shopping precinct that killed twenty people and injured twice that number. Klaus was not interested in Hilary's ideas but in his money. Hilary was not interested in Klaus so much as in his NLG associates, who seemed to him as fascinatingly dangerous as panthers, perfect associates for somebody named Hilary Engels Mannering. It was through Klaus that Hilary got in touch with young men and women of similar beliefs in Britain. He did not take them on trust. Each of them was required to perform an illegal act — arson, theft, violent robbery — before acceptance into the BPB. What did BPB stand for? The Beatrix Potter Brigade.

It was of course Hilary who had chosen the ludicrous name, and he had gone further, giving members of the group names of characters in the stories and insisting that they should wear appropriate masks when carrying out group exploits. Among their achievements were a bomb planted in a cabinet minister's house (it exploded, but unfortunately everybody was out), a fire bomb that had burned down most of a large London hotel, and a wages theft from London Airport. Hilary himself stayed in the background, interviewing possible new recruits and setting them tests which some refused to undertake. He would then explain that he was a theatrical producer who had been testing their reactions (which was true enough in a way), and pay them off with a ten-pound note. The enterprise had the elements of theatricality and childishness that he loved, and for three years now it had completely absorbed him.

On the afternoon of the unsuccessful attempt in Kensington Gardens, the members of the group gathered in an extension of Mannering's wine cellars that ran below the Thames near London Bridge. They entered by a door in an alley, which led to a passage and a storeroom. In the storeroom a perfectly camouflaged door led to a single large, windowless room. There were wine racks along two walls, with dusty bottles in them. On the other walls were prints of Beatrix Potter characters — the cat Simpkin buying food for the tailor of Gloucester, Mrs. Tiggy-Winkle the hedgehog in her kitchen, Pigling Bland on the way to market, and of course Peter Rabbit, who was shown escaping from Farmer McGregor's attempt to catch him with a sieve. The ceiling was low and the lighting came from lamps invisibly sunk into it, so that the effect was one of mysterious gloom. There was only one visible door, which was said to lead directly to the Thames.

"It's romantic," Klaus Dongen had said when he saw it. "And ridiculous."

"And safe," Hilary had replied.

There were ten of them besides Hilary, and he waited until they all arrived, refusing to listen when both Peter Rabbit and Simpkin tried to tell him what had happened. Hilary was now in his late thirties, a tall, thin man with a sharp nose and a mouth perpetually turned down at the corners as though he had just tasted something bitter. He was older than the rest of them, and although his fluting voice had something absurd about it, he seemed in some indefinable way dangerous. His restlessness, his jerky movements, the sudden grimaces intended as laughs, all gave the impression that he was inhabited by some violent spirit which he was only just able to keep under control.

"Now that we are all here," he said at last, "I should like a report on what happened. Peter, you were in charge of the operation."

The thick-set blond young man said, "It was a plant; they must have been on to it the whole time. It's a bloody miracle we all got away."

Hilary sighed gently. "That is hardly the way to present a report, Peter — "

"My name's not Peter. I'm sick of playing kids' games." There was a murmur of agreement. "If you'd set this up properly — "

"Is that the way it goes? You're blaming me, yet you are incapable even of presenting a report on what went wrong."

"How can you present a report on a disaster?" He stared down at the table as though he were a discontented schoolboy, and he looked remarkably like Charlie Ramsden.

Hilary pinched out the end of a Russian cigarette, used a long, narrow lighter and puffed blue smoke. "Since you are unable or unwilling to present a report, I must do so myself."

"You weren't there," said the tramp who had been feeding pigeons.

"Really, Squirrel Nutkin? Would you like me to describe the man you hit when you got away?" The tramp looked at him unbelievingly. "I was on the seventh floor of a building almost opposite, watching through binoculars."

"But not present," somebody said.

"Not present, as you say. The directing mind should be separate from the executive hand. But let us examine the affair from the beginning. It was suggested by a foreign colleague that we should take the son of the Duke of Milchester and hold him for ransom. The sum asked would be a quarter of a million pounds, which the Duke could comfortably have paid by selling a couple of pictures. Now let me tell you the object of this — to use a piece of deplorable American slang — snatch. Why do we want the money? It is to give financial backing for a project to be undertaken from overseas by a very, *very* famous person. Can you guess?"

"The Wolf." The pretty girl who had sat on the bench with the blond young man breathed the words reverently. And reverence was in order. The Wolf was the most famous terrorist in the world, a man who killed with impersonal detachment, and had never been known to refuse a job if the fee was big enough.

"Well done, Pigwig." Hilary smiled, but even his smile was acid. "But it is not wise to use that name. I shall call him Mr McGregor, the ruler of all the little Flopsy Bunnies and squirrels and mice and pigs. And do you know Mr McGregor's target, his projected target?"

"One of the newspaper owners?" Squirrel Nutkin suggested.

"A politician? The Chancellor, the Prime Minister?" That was Pigwig.

Hilary shook his head. "Look higher."

"You don't mean —"

"Oh, but I do. Mr McGregor will be aiming at — what shall I call it — the highest in the land."

There was a gasp around the table. Again Hilary gave them his acid smile. Then the blond young man said, "But it all went wrong; we couldn't even get the kidnapping right. Why should the Wolf think we can set up an almost impossible job when we've fallen down on this one?"

"The Wolf — Mr McGregor — sets up his own jobs, as you call them. We should be his paymaster, nothing more. But as you say, this exercise went wrong. We had not one but two dress rehearsals, and you knew exactly what the nanny looked like. So what happened?"

"The baby wasn't the Duke's. It was pitch black."

"That's right. I looked into the pram, I saw it." Pigwig nodded agreement.

"They knew what we were doing and substituted the baby. And you can see what that means." The thrust of his jaw, the jutting of his chin, were really very reminiscent of Charlie Ramsden.

Hilary rose, walked quickly and silently over to a cupboard above the wine racks and opened it to reveal glasses and, in a refrigerated section, several bottles of champagne. This was a ritual. When they assembled at the cellars there would always be champagne in the cupboard, and it was always Moët & Chandon of a good year. Pigwig, one of the group's newer members, had thought of saying that she would prefer whisky, but had decided against it.

The corks came out, the champagne was poured. Hilary raised his glass.

"I drink to Mr McGregor. And to the success of his mission. When he comes."

"But he won't be coming now, will he? As you said, he only works for cash." That was the man in the black jacket and striped trousers, an unnoticeable sandy fellow with a toothbrush moustache.

"Very true, Simpkin. But in the meantime we have a problem. The conclusion from what happened is simple and unmistakable."

"Somebody grassed." It was the only other woman round the table who spoke. She was in her late twenties, had a knife scar on her cheek and a heavy, ruthless face. It had been a touch of irony on Hilary's part to name her after the genial hedgehog Mrs Tiggy-Winkle.

"Again I deplore the use of slang, but it expresses a truth. Traitor, Judas, grass — it does not matter what name we use. The fact is that one of us must have told the authorities. Or told somebody else, who gave us away. Did any of you tell a friend, a lover, a wife, a husband?" Nobody spoke. "Just so. It is as I feared."

"There's one queer thing," Simpkin said. "If the counter-espionage boys were tipped off, why weren't they all over the place, why let us get away? Isn't it possible that it was a genuine change of plan, and we were just unlucky?"

"With a *black* baby, Simpkin? I should like to think that was true, but a black baby! Somebody was playing a joke on us."

"I know who it was," Peter Rabbit said. He pointed across the table at Simpkin. "You."

"And how does Peter Rabbit make that out?" There was an undercurrent of mockery in Hilary's voice, but he did not fail to notice that Simpkin was left sitting at one end of the table, the others drawing away as though he had an infectious disease. Simpkin himself seemed unaffected. He drained the glass in front of him, and refilled it from one of the bottles on the table.

"I'll tell you how I know," Peter Rabbit began in a low, furious voice. Hilary stopped him. His eyes were bright with pleasure.

"We must do this according to law. There was no trial in any Beatrix Potter story — "

"Sod the Beatrix Potter stories," said the man who had been leaning against the lamppost, a youth whose spottiness was partly hidden by his thick beard.

"Now then, Samuel Whiskers, no bad language *if* you please," Hilary said indulgently.

The young man who had been pushing a broom spoke. He was another recent recruit, a broad-shouldered figure with a round ruddy face and a snoutish, vertical-nostrilled nose which had led Hilary to christen him Pigling Bland. Like all of them except Peter Rabbit and Hilary himself, he spoke in the mid-Atlantic accent that denies the existence of English class distinctions.

"He's right. We don't want any playing about. If there's a grass, we've got to know who it is."

"Precisely, Pigling. But let us do it by considering evidence rather than simple accusation. Simpkin, you are the accused; you may remain where you are. Peter Rabbit, you will be prosecutor; you should go to the other side of the table. The rest of you will serve as the jury and should group yourselves at the end. Thank you. I will serve as judge, summing up the evidence, although the verdict will be yours. I think I should sit away from you. Over here, perhaps." He placed his chair beside the door. "If you wish, Simpkin, you may ask one of the jury to defend you."

"I'll defend myself," Simpkin said. Of all the people in the room, he seemed the least moved.

"Very well. Prosecuting counsel, begin."

The blond young man did not look at Hilary. "I should like to say that this is a stupid way — "

Hilary tapped on the arm of his chair with the lighter he was using for another cigarette. "Out of order. Produce your evidence."

"All right. Simpkin joined the group four months ago. Since then he's been concerned in three jobs. The first was leaving a bomb in an Underground train. He did that himself. At least he says so, but the bomb never went off. Did he ever leave it?"

Simpkin intervened. "Can I answer that?"

"Not now. You'll have your turn." Hilary's eyes had been closed, and now he shut them again. With eyes closed, Peter Rabbit's voice sounded exactly like Charlie Ramsden's.

"Two. Simpkin was one of the people who planned to get a comrade out of Brixton Prison. Almost at the last minute the comrade was moved to Parkhurst. Coincidence? Perhaps. Three. A couple of weeks ago, we should have had an open-and-shut job, getting documents out of a ministry file. They'd have been very useful to us. You, Jeremy Fisher" — he nodded at a man who had been driving one of the getaway cars — "I don't know your name, so I have to call you that — you set it up; you had a friend on the inside. Simpkin is supposed to know the ministry layout, which is why he was involved so closely. The job went through all right, but the papers weren't in the file.

"And four, the job today. You were the grass."

He stopped. Hilary opened his eyes. "Is that all?"

"No. But I'd like to hear what he has to say."

Simpkin's features were watchful; he really did look a little like the cat he was supposed to represent. "No need to say much. One, I left the bomb. The mechanism was faulty; it was reported in the press."

"Of course. You fixed a cover story."

Simpkin shrugged. "Number two was a coincidence, must have been. Number three, maybe the papers had been taken out months earlier. Anyway, why pick on me; why not Jeremy Fisher?"

"He wasn't in on the other jobs. You were."

"So were you." Simpkin permitted himself a brief catlike smile. "And if you remember, I was against this snatch. I thought it was too risky."

"I'm an old member, not a new one. We've made mistakes before, but it's since you joined us that things have been going wrong persistently. And of course you'd be against the snatch; that was another bit of cover."

Hilary moved in his chair. "You said there was something more."

"Yes. Some of you know that I have — that I see people — "

"We know about your social position," Mrs Tiggy-Winkle said in her harsh voice. "We know you meet the best people. I've seen your name in the papers."

"All right," Peter Rabbit said. "Through my position I've been able to get a good deal of information. You know that," he said to Hilary, who nodded and smiled his acid smile. "Last Wednesday I had dinner at Horton's, which is a small luncheon and dining club with a very restricted membership. Top people in the services and the ministries, a few members of the government and so on."

"Top people, period," Mrs Tiggy-Winkle said. "Nice company you keep."

The young man ignored her. "Horton's has a couple of rooms where you can take people for dinner if you've got something extremely private to discuss. On this night — it was fairly late, very few people in the club — three people came out of one of these rooms. One was Giles Ravelin, who's an assistant head in MI6. He's a member of Horton's, and the two others must have been his guests. One was Sir Llewellyn Scott, who acts as a sort of link man between the police and the counterespionage agencies. And the third was Simpkin." He paused. "I want him to explain how he came to be there. If he can."

It was for such moments as these that Hilary lived, moments of excitement outside the routine of life. Revolutionary intrigue he had found for the most part boring, a matter of dull little men discussing how to obtain power over other dull little men. But the possible visit of the Wolf, the fun of calling him Mr McGregor, the tension in this long, low windowless room with its hidden light that made every face look ghostly pale — oh, these were the moments that made life worth living, whatever their outcome. How would Simpkin react to Charlie Ramsden — no, to Peter Rabbit? What would he say?

The silence was total. All of them were staring at Simpkin, waiting for Simpkin. At last he gave a faint, catlike cough. "What was the light like?"

"The *light*?" Then he realised the question's purpose. "A good deal better than it is here. Good enough to recognise you."

"How near were you to this man?"

"I was four feet away or less, sitting in an alcove. You didn't see me, or I don't think so, because I was partly hidden. But I had a good view of you."

"You saw the man for how long? Two seconds?"

"Long enough. It was you. I'll ask you again. What were you doing there; who do you work for?"

From the rest of them, those appointed as a jury, there came a murmur, an angry dangerous sound. "Answer him," Samuel Whiskers said. "If you don't, we'll know what to think."

"I can't answer," Simpkin said flatly. "I wasn't there." There was a moment's pause while they digested this. "I was never inside that place in my life, never heard of it. I gave him a chance to say he was mistaken, but he didn't take it. He's lying."

The two men looked at each other across the table. "You bloody Judas, you won't get out of it like that," Peter Rabbit said.

Hilary steepled his fingers and offered a judge's comment. "It comes to this, then: that we have an accusation but no proof."

"You said it was last Wednesday. What time did this meeting take place?" the pretty girl known as Pigwig asked.

"Between ten and ten-thirty at night."

"You're sure it was Wednesday, certain that was the day?"

As Peter Rabbit said he was sure, Simpkin seemed suddenly to wake from a brown study and showed his first sign of emotion, almost shouting at her to keep out of this, it wasn't her affair. She disregarded him.

"Last Wednesday, Bill — "

"You are not to use personal names," Hilary cried. "Pseudonyms *must* be preserved."

"What stupid game are you playing; who do you think you're kidding?" she screamed at him. "Half of us know who the others are and what they do, and those who don't could easily find out. At ten o'clock last Wednesday Bill wasn't at any Horton's Club or whatever it's called. He was in bed with me, had been all evening. Around eight I got up and made scrambled eggs, then we went back to bed."

"Is that true?" Hilary asked Simpkin, who shrugged and then nodded. "Two different stories. They can't both be right."

The round-faced young man called Pigling Bland said, "No, they can't. And I know who's telling the truth. A couple of days ago, I saw him — Peter Rabbit — walking along Piccadilly. He was with somebody who looked familiar, though I couldn't place him. But I knew who it was as soon as I heard his name today, because I've seen his picture in the papers often enough. It was this Scott, Llewellyn Scott."

"You're sure?"

"I can't prove it, can I? But yes, I'm sure."

"Does anybody else wish to speak? Very well. You have heard the evidence, and I don't think there's any need for a judicial summing up. Members of the jury, will those of you who find Simpkin guilty put up your hands." No hand was raised. "Simpkin, you are acquitted."

"That's not the end of it," Mrs Tiggy-Winkle said. "He's the grass." She pointed at Peter Rabbit, who seemed suddenly as isolated as Simpkin had been.

"He was lying. He must be the grass — stands to reason." That was Samuel Whiskers.

"Do you wish to pass a verdict on Peter Rabbit?"

"I certainly do. Guilty." Mrs Tiggy-Winkle's face was grim. The scar on it pulsed red.

"How many of you agree with her? Put up your hands." They all went up except Simpkin's. "Simpkin?"

"I just think he made a mistake. No need to suppose anything else."

"Then who do you think grassed on us?" Samuel Whiskers shouted. Simpkin gave one of his characteristic shrugs.

"Peter Rabbit, you have been found guilty without a single dissentient vote. Have you anything to say?"

The blond young man passed a hand through his hair in a gesture intolerably reminiscent of Charlie Ramsden, and cried out in bewilderment. "I don't know what's happening. This is all crazy, Hilary. You know me. You know it is."

"No names, Peter. You know the rules," Hilary said gently. He got up from his chair, walked over to the young man, held out his pack of Russian cigarettes. "Let's talk about it."

"I'll smoke my own." Peter Rabbit shook one from a pack, put it in his mouth.

"Here's a light." Flame shot up from the long, narrow lighter, and smoke came from the cigarette. Peter Rabbit looked at Hilary in total astonishment. He put a hand to his neck. The cigarette fell out of his mouth. He dropped to the floor.

Simpkin stood up. Somebody gave a cry, sharply cut off. Hilary giggled and held up the lighter.

"I got it from one of the NLG boys. An ordinary lighter; you've seen me using it. But if you press a button at the bottom a dart comes out." He pressed it and a tiny thing, hardly thicker than a needle, buried itself in Peter Rabbit's body in the wall poster. "Very effective."

"Nobody said kill him," Samuel Whiskers said.

"The verdict was yours. There was only one possible sentence."

"But he'd been in the group as long as me, as long as any of us."

"There are no medals for long service." Hilary gave his acid smile. "This door leads to a chute that will deposit Peter Rabbit in the Thames. If one of you will give me a hand, we can dispose of our grass. Then I suggest that we sit down and consider some new plans for raising the necessary cash to bring Mr McGregor over here."

Simpkin helped him out with the body. They stood together while it slid down the chute and vanished. When they returned, an obituary on Peter Rabbit was pronounced by Mrs Tiggy-Winkle.

"Good riddance to bad rubbish," she said.

EPILOGUE

Just after three o'clock on the following afternoon, Simpkin, whose name was Bill Gray, entered an office block in Shaftesbury Avenue, took the lift up to the third floor and went through a frosted-glass door lettered *Inter-European Holidays*, *Travel Consultants*. He nodded to the girl in reception and walked down a corridor to a room at the end. There, in a small office with three telephones in it, including one with a direct line to Giles Ravelin, he found Jean Conybeare and Derek Johnson — alias Pigwig and Pigling Bland — waiting for him.

"My God, what a shambles," Derek said.

"Macabre." Jean shivered. "He enjoyed it, that Hilary Mannering. He's a real creep."

"It was a bad scene," Derek went on. "If it hadn't been for Jean here, I don't know what might have happened. 'He was in bed with me, had been all evening,'" he said falsetto. "Wonderful."

"You provided the clincher, Derek, with that story about meeting him in the street."

Derek Johnson shook his head. "Poor bloody Peter Rabbit — it was a clincher for him, all right. It was just his bad luck, Bill, that he saw you coming out of that room with Ravelin and Scott."

Bill Gray was at his desk looking through papers about Operation Wolfhunt. Now he looked up. "No need for tears. He was just an upper-class twit who got himself mixed up with a gang of thugs."

"Mannering isn't a thug, he's a psychopath," Jean said. "The *pleasure* he took in using that lighter! I hate to be in the same room with him." She asked curiously, "Did you know he'd seen you at Horton's?"

"I was afraid he might have done."

"So what would you have done if I'd not come up with that story?"

"Shot it out. But that would have wrecked the operation."

"Mannering should be in a padded cell."

"No argument. But let me remind you that if we take in his crackpot Beatrix Potter Group, we lose a chance of catching the Wolf. That's the object of the operation, remember? Now, we couldn't let them get away with kidnapping a duke's son, though I was able to make sure everybody got clear. They still have to raise funds to get the Wolf over here, and we've got to help."

They waited. Bill Gray's catlike features were intent; he might have been about to pounce. "I think this is going to come best from you, Derek. You've got a friend who's a watchman in a bank in Cheapside. He'll provide duplicate keys. There's wads of money in the vaults; we knock out the watchman and pay him off, collect the cash. The money will be slush, but they won't need to use much of it until they pay out the Wolf, and I'll put the word around so that in the meantime anything they use will be honoured. We'll talk about the details, Derek, after I've set it up. Then you can go to Mannering and talk about it. The Wolf's said to be in the Argentine at the moment, but he's in touch with an NLG man there and we have some contacts with him. When he knows that his fee's going to be paid, he'll come over."

"And until then?"

A smile touched Bill Gray's face and was gone like winter sunshine. "Until then we're waiting for Mr McGregor."

PRIVATE GORMAN'S LUCK

Peter Lovesey

As Private Gorman saw it, he was dead unlucky.

He had just been picked up by the redcaps for the seventh time. He couldn't stand the army. The snag was that he was no more of a success at deserting than he was at rifle drill. On four occasions he had got only a couple of miles from the barrack gates. Twice they had collected him from his home in Bermondsey. But the latest attempt was his most ambitious. He had managed three days on the run and all but got away. His assessment of the experience in the quiet of his cell in Hounslow Barracks was that only his stinking luck had let him down.

At first, fortune had favoured him. After two nights sleeping rough, his uniform had got too shabby to wear with confidence, so he had started to look for some civvies. He was passing a bomb site in Hounslow when he spotted a damaged house across the street. It was like looking into a doll's house; the blast had ripped away the entire front. The wardens had cleared the floor downstairs, but the upper floor was unsafe, so everything was left: two bedrooms with beds, chests of drawers, wardrobes, dressing-tables and — of surpassing interest to Gorman — a blue double-breasted suit on a hanger suspended from the top of one of the wardrobe doors.

That evening in the blackout (as he told it later to Private Plumridge, who was on fatigues in the guardroom), Gorman had gone back to the house and waited nearby for an air raid to create a distraction. This was the summer of 1944, when the flying bombs were at their worst, so there was a fair chance of the siren going some time. When it did, and Gorman heard the steady drone of a V1 coming over from London, he made his move. The buzzbombs held no fears for Gorman. He had a firm conviction that he was safe from those things, however close they came. His enemy wasn't Hitler; it was the redcaps. He hopped over the rubble, through the path cleared by the wardens, into the dining-room, out to the hall and up the stairs. As easy as ABC.

For the first time in his army career, he was glad of his metal-studded boots when he got up there and found the bedroom door locked by some security-minded bastard from the rescue service. Two good kicks and he was inside.

Then it was a matter of keeping close to the wall and edging around the room to the dark shape of the wardrobe. He stepped deftly over one of the fallen chairs, sidled past the dressing table and reached out his fingertips to feel for the suit. With his hand firmly over the padded shoulder, he lifted it from the wardrobe and held it against his chest. The sleeve length matched his arm to perfection. Elated, he started back around the edge of the room, blundered into the chair, went arse over tip, as he put it to Private Plumridge, and plunged alarmingly to the floor.

There was a short, uncomfortable hiatus, not unlike the seconds after a flying bomb cuts out, when Private Gorman waited for the crash. It started as a rending sound in the plaster, followed by a crack and a groan as the entire floor caved in. Gorman dropped yelling with a mass of wood, plaster and linoleum. His first thought was that the entire building would collapse on him.

After the fall, he heard himself spluttering, so he reckoned he was still alive. Most of his body had hit the mattress of the double bed. One of his legs hurt and he couldn't breathe for plaster in the air, but he was able to get up. Still holding the precious suit, he stumbled through the debris and hobbled off in the blackout as quickly as his injured leg would let him.

He passed the night at the feet of an angel in a churchyard, with the suit laid out on a granite tomb nearby. At first light, he gave himself a fitting. For off-the-peg, it was as good as anything from the Fifty Shilling Tailors. Better. In the pockets there was four and threepence, a packet of Senior Service and a box of Swan Vestas. After he had dumped his uniform under a heap of discarded wreaths and flowers, Gorman climbed over the churchyard wall into someone's garden and helped himself to a shirt from the washing line. Without clothing coupons, what else was he to do?

A smoke, a shave at a barber's in Hounslow High Street and a cup of tea at the bus station gave him the confidence he needed to enter the town hall and see the National Registration people about an identity card. If you said you had lost your card, it cost a shilling to apply for a replacement, and they would give you a receipt that you could show to anyone who challenged you. A passport to civilian life.

Gorman understood identity numbers. When the woman clerk asked him, he rattled off a number similar to his own before he was called up, AB to say he lived in the London Borough of Bermondsey, and a slight variation in the digits after, to prevent her from tracking him to his real address. He gave a false name. He was getting smart at last.

When the clerk asked him for the shilling, Gorman casually took a two-shilling piece from his pocket and placed it on the counter. She wrote out the receipt, stamped it, handed it to Gorman and passed him his shilling change. And that was when his luck ran out.

In his elation, he dropped the shilling. It fell off the counter and rolled for a short distance across the floor. Gorman pursued it. He put out his foot to step on it just as someone stooped to pick it up. With his regulation army boots Gorman crushed the fingers of the police constable on duty.

No apology could save him. He was unable to explain how a civilian in a smart blue suit came to be wearing metal-studded army boots. Inside the hour, he was collected by the redcaps.

"I was dead unlucky," he complained once more to Private Plumridge.

"Deplorably unfortunate," agreed Plumridge, who was socially a cut above Gorman. Plumridge was regularly in trouble for insubordination when addressing NCOs, who were apt to mistake an elegant turn of phrase for sarcasm. It was a shame he had failed the intelligence test for officer selection, yet to his credit he had come to terms with the rigours of life in the ranks. He had no plans to desert. "To be candid with you, Gorman, I'm at a loss to understand why you keep doing it."

Gorman scowled. "I hate the army, don't I?"

Plumridge leaned on the polisher he was supposed to be using on the floor outside Gorman's cell. "If it comes to that, I'm not passionately devoted to wearing khaki and living in wooden huts myself."

"Why do you stick it, then?" asked Gorman, expecting a short sermon about King and Country and Mr Churchill.

A smug smile spread across Plumridge's face. "I have an incentive. A certain somebody who happens to believe I'm the finest soldier in the British army."

"God Almighty, who's that?"

Plumridge lifted one of the flaps of his fatigue dress and took out a photograph, which he pushed through the grille of the cell door. "Annabelle."

Gorman studied the picture and passed it back. "Not bad. Not bad at all. Your girl?"

"Wife, in point of fact," Plumridge remarked with an attempt to be casual.

"You're married?" Gorman said in a shrill note. "Give us another look at that."

Plumridge held the picture up. "She is rather fetching, I must admit. She agreed to marry me the day my call-up papers arrived. She adores the uniform, you see. Before that, I was merely one of a string of would-be suitors. Now Annabelle is keeping my home fire burning in Chiddingfold."

"Where's that?"

"In a rather select part of Surrey that you wouldn't have heard of. Whenever I get a weekend pass, I'm off there. She's terribly proud of me. Fully expects me to get a stripe before Christmas." He took the photograph away from the grille and gazed at it. "So you see, I'm utterly committed to the army."

The conversation was cut short by the appearance of Corporal Harker, the Military Policeman on duty. Harker was the most conscientious redcap in the barracks. "What's that in your grubby fist, soldier?"

"Only a photograph, corporal," answered Plumridge, tucking it away.

Harker snapped his fingers and held out his hand.

Plumridge reluctantly handed over the picture of Annabelle. "My wife, actually."

"My wife, actually, *corporal*."

"Sorry, corporal." Plumridge hesitated. "May I have it back please? It's rather precious."

Harker snorted his displeasure. "You've got no business showing photographs of women to the prisoner. He's under close arrest and you're supposed to be polishing the floor. What else have you been handing over? Cigarettes? Chocolate? Turn out your pockets, at the double."

Plumridge obeyed, producing a letter addressed to Annabelle, his pay book, a set of keys and his identity disc.

"This should be round your neck, not in your pocket," Harker reprimanded him. "CO's orders: identity discs will be worn by all personnel at all times so long as the air raids continue. That means round your fat neck, Plumridge, have you got that?"

"Yes, corporal."

"Put it on, then. Put this other rubbish back in your pockets and get polishing the floor. I'm going to search the prisoner now, and if I find so much as a peppermint on his person, you're on a charge, do you understand?"

Plumridge nodded unhappily.

The search of Private Gorman was a simple matter because he was wearing only shorts and a singlet, having disposed of his uniform and been deprived of the blue civilian suit. To his credit, he was still wearing his identity disc around his neck. Corporal Harker could find nothing irregular, so he had to content himself with some disparaging remarks about deserters, and, when he emerged from the cell, a blistering attack on the quality of Plumridge's polishing. He ordered Plumridge to buff the entire floor again, and with that he went off duty.

"That man's an absolute sadist," Plumridge confided through the grille to Gorman.

"Who's on duty now?"

"The tall ginger one with the moustache."

"That's Corporal Davis. He's all right. He'll let you off in twenty minutes."

This might have been the case, but inside three minutes, the air raid warning sounded and within seconds they could hear the ominous note of a flying bomb. The procedure in an air raid was to evacuate the guard room, which was a timber structure, and go into the underground shelter at the rear. Corporal Davis unlocked Gorman's cell. He was holding a pair of handcuffs.

"Let's have your wrist."

"Sounds like a close one, corp," commented Gorman, untroubled and glad of the distraction.

In accordance with standing orders, Corporal Davis manacled Gorman to himself and shouted to Plumridge to go with them. The entrance to the shelter was about thirty yards away, across a stretch of grass. Before they were through the back door of the guard room. Gorman heard the engine of the V1 cut out. He looked up.

It was diving straight towards them out of a brilliant blue sky, its black and green camouflage clearly visible on the upper fuselage, its stubby, squared-off wings and tail giving it the look of an aircraft crudely manufactured for destruction, its propulsion unit spurting orange flames.

Corporal Davis yelled, "Come on!" to Plumridge, who was last out of the door. Gorman, his injured leg forgotten, was already halfway across the grass towards the shelter, jerking Davis with him.

The flying bomb didn't actually hit the guard room. It crashed into the tarmac just in front of the main gates. The blast ripped the guard room and the armoury apart. Slats of wood hailed down.

Gorman was temporarily deafened, but unhurt. He had made it to the sandbags heaped outside the shelter and leapt over into the dug-out front as the explosion happened. His arm was still draped over the sandbags, attached to Corporal Davis. He tugged on it and felt no response. He hauled himself up and over the sandbags.

Corporal Davis had been hit by some piece of flying debris. He was either stunned or dead. Gorman didn't wait to check. Someone else's misfortune was his opportunity. He felt for the chain attached to Davis's belt, found the key of the handcuffs and released himself. He was about to desert for the eighth time.

He looked around him. Black smoke was blotting out the sky. The wreckage of the guard room had caught fire and the long grass at the rear was smouldering. It would probably be safe to go out by the main gate. The blokes on sentry duty must have been blasted to kingdom come.

As he stepped forward, he almost tripped over a body in fatigue dress. Private Plumridge was dead, dead beyond argument, with half his head blown off. Gorman's first impulse was to hare away and he had already gone a couple of paces when the thought occurred to him that Plumridge's fatigue dress might be of use. He knew from experience that nights in the open could be cold, even in August, and he didn't relish sleeping rough, dressed as he was.

He braced himself for another look at the body. The jacket was soiled with blood and ripped in a couple of places, but worth taking if there was time, and the trousers were perfectly usable. When it came to deserting, Gorman wasn't squeamish about robbing the living or the dead. So he unbuttoned the clothes and peeled them off, leaving Plumridge in singlet and shorts, just as he was himself.

Then he had his brainwave.

It was sparked by the sight of Plumridge's identity disc. The opportunity was there to free himself totally from the army. If he removed Plumridge's disc and replaced it with his own, everyone would assume that 505918 Gorman, Private E. was dead. They wouldn't be able to identify the body by looking at the face, because most of it was missing. And in a few minutes, the grass where Plumridge was lying would be alight, charring him all over.

While he was switching the discs, Gorman thought of an extra refinement. He ran back to Corporal Davis's body, dragged it the few yards across the turf and positioned it alongside Plumridge. Then he clipped the spare handcuff over Plumridge's wrist. The clincher, he told himself, grinning. That done, he grabbed the fatigue dress and dashed across the smouldering grass to freedom.

*

Soon after, the army tackled the job of putting out the fires and recovering the bodies. There were four dead and they were identified as Privates Harris and Parks, the two men on guard at the main gate, Corporal Davis of the Military Police and the prisoner, Private Gorman. Next of kin were informed.

After some hours, there was concern about the welfare of Private Plumridge, who was known to have been detailed to perform fatigues in the guard room and who appeared to be missing. A thorough examination of the debris failed to reveal a fifth body. Searches of the surrounding area were organised and a trail of footsteps was discovered leading from the charred area where two of the bodies had been found towards the main gate. It was assumed that Plumridge had wandered off, possibly in a state of concussion, and the civilian police were informed. Two days later, his identity disc was found by a man walking his dog on Hounslow Heath.

Plumridge's wife Annabelle was contacted, but she informed Corporal Harker, the Military Policeman who called on her in Chiddingfold, that she had heard nothing from him. She seemed mystified, but not unduly distressed by her husband's disappearance.

A week passed, and there was no further news of Plumridge. The funerals of the four men killed by the flying bomb were all attended by senior officers. Ten days after the tragedy, a service of remembrance was conducted by the padre.

After the service, the CO called at the temporary, prefabricated guard room and spoke to Corporal Harker. He expressed concern about the lack of information concerning Private Plumridge. He detested the very idea, but he felt obliged to consider the possibility that Plumridge had taken advantage of the bombing to go absent without leave. After questioning Harker closely about the reaction of Annabelle Plumridge to her husband's disappearance, he authorised Harker to make a second visit to Chiddingfold and see whether the lady could throw any more light on the mystery.

The same ten days had been a testing time for Private Gorman. To his credit, it was the longest period he had spent on the run.

Yet without civilian clothes or even a passable uniform, he had been compelled to spend the days in hiding and the nights scavenging. He was living mainly on raw eggs and vegetables stolen from suburban gardens. It was much too soon after his supposed demise to think of going home. At the sight of him, his mother would scream and his father would tell the whole of Bermondsey and Rotherhithe that a miracle had happened.

He sat hunched in his latest hide-out, a dilapidated boat shed at Twickenham, ironically trying to lift his spirits with what the army called planning. What he needed urgently was a set of clothes and some money. It was no use trusting to luck. He couldn't expect to come across another bomb site with a suit on a hanger waiting for him to collect. As for money, Plumridge hadn't left so much as a halfpenny in the pockets of the fatigue dress. Just the pay book, and what use was that to a deserter? Gorman had torn it into small pieces and thrown it out days ago, with the letter to Annabelle. Apart from the clothes, the only things of Plumridge's still in his possession were two keys on a ring, one that probably fitted the padlock of his locker, the other a Yale which had come in useful for scraping the dirt off carrots and parsnips. He had since picked up a knife, so the keys could be chucked out as well now. There was small chance of finding a lock they would open.

Or was there?

As he dangled the key ring on his finger, Gorman had another of his brainwaves. Wasn't it reasonable to suppose that the Yale was the key to Plumridge's house in Surrey, and wouldn't it be worth finding the place and seeing if it fitted? There was sure to be clothes there, and food and probably money. This was the luck he needed, and all this time he had been carrying it around with him!

Where was it that Plumridge had said he lived? The address had been on that blasted letter. Victoria House — it had struck Gorman as comical, Plums at Victoria House — but what the hell was the name of the village? Chittyfield? Chiddingfield? Not quite.

Chiddingfold! Victoria House, Chiddingfold.

It wasn't easy to find the place. Surrey was a large county, and signposts had been removed to frustrate troop movements in the event of an invasion. He headed south, away from London, reasoning that it must be out of the surburban reaches. Going through Hampton Court on the first night, he broke into three cars parked outside a pub before he found what he needed: a county map.

Chiddingfold was near Haslemere on the Sussex border, too far to reach in a night, so he walked the twenty miles to Guildford, and laid up in some outbuildings at a farm just south of the town. He found apples stored there in boxes, and ate enough to satisfy hunger and thirst in one.

The following night was a Saturday and a full moon, so he was glad he had not left too many miles to cover, because people would be out later than usual. It was after eleven when he started, and half-past two in the morning when he finally located Victoria House. Happily, it was a detached building in its own grounds. No telephone wires were visible. He had no wish to disturb Annabelle Plumridge's sleep if he could avoid it, but it was a relief to know that she couldn't call the police.

The first thing was to see whether the key fitted. He started up the drive towards the house.

In bed, Annabelle heard the crunch of gravel outside. "Listen!"

"What's the matter?"

"Just listen, Simon. There's someone outside!"

"A fox, I expect."

"No, it's too heavy for that. He's by the front door! Oh, God, what if it's my husband!"

Corporal Harker swung his legs to the floor and pulled on a pair of shorts. He went to the chair over which he had draped his uniform and drew his baton from its sheath. Then he glided out of the door and downstairs.

Annabelle shrank back in bed, pulling the sheet tight around her neck. She heard the sound of a key turning in the door, a shout of surprise and then a crack that made her gasp with terror, followed by two more, then silence.

The suspense was petrifying before the landing light came on, and Corporal Harker stood in the doorway holding his baton. "I'm afraid I had to hit him," he said, breathing heavily.

"Charlie? My husband?" whispered Annabelle.

He hesitated. "Private Plumridge, yes. You don't have to come downstairs. I can deal with it."

"Is he. . . .?"

"I'm afraid so."

"Oh, my poor Charlie!" Annabelle started to sob.

"Come off it," Corporal Harker said in the sharp voice of authority he used in the guard room. "You told me you couldn't bear to live with a deserter. You said you fancied me in my red cap and white gaiters."

"I know, but. . . ."

"He must have had a thin skull. Some people do. It's better this way. Your reputation, my career."

"But what shall we do with him?"

"Easy. You don't have to do a thing. Better if you stay up here. I'll put him in the van and take him with me. I know a couple of bomb sites on the way back to barracks. I'll hide him under some rubble, and even if they find him, no one will ever guess who he was, or how it happened."

"I suppose it was just bad luck," Annabelle said to appease her feelings of shock.

"That's right," Corporal Harker confirmed. "He was unlucky. Dead unlucky."

ANNIVERSARY

Margaret Yorke

It was a special day.

Mrs Frobisher had made careful preparations. A bottle of champagne was on ice and she had bought smoked salmon, asparagus, and a plump partridge.

In the living room of her comfortable flat all was arranged. The table was laid with the best silver and cut glass. There were spring flowers in a small vase.

She would celebrate alone, for next to the money her tranquil solitude was, after so long, a prize. For three years she had steadfastly carried out her daily duties — fetching and carrying, wheeling Matthew out in his chair, placing his tweed hat tenderly on his pale bald head, wrapping his soft wool scarf round his throat (though she longed to pull it tight against his windpipe), tucking a mohair rug round his knees and his bony old ankles. Because of her his last years had been spent in great comfort — and, indeed, he owed them to her nursing skill.

They met when the agency sent her as his special nurse to the nursing home where Matthew was recovering from a stroke. She was accustomed to caring for the elderly, and she had found him an easy patient. He was light to lift and determined to regain his powers of speech and movement. Aiding his rehabilitation had been a challenge to her skills. After months in the nursing home, he was well enough to leave but required full-time home care, and he suggested to her that she should become his permanent attendant.

This might be her only chance: she had resolved not to let it pass. She was a plain, sturdy woman with a sallow complexion and glasses. Her legs were stout and her ankles thick — though her feet were small, and often, for this reason, ached as they carried her heavy body about her duties. Mr Frobisher was a widower, and wealthy. His visitors at the nursing home had been his former business associates — he had retired from active work before his illness but was still on the board of several companies. He had no children.

Once home in the flat overlooking the esplanade he became demanding, and she worked hard complying with his wishes. She kept him physically spruce and arranged bridge evenings for him with former cronies, for he had recovered enough to enjoy a few rubbers once or twice a week. She would slip out, then, for a couple of hours at the cinema, returning in time to serve drinks and sandwiches to the men. Otherwise, apart from shopping and trips to the library, she went out only with Matthew, pushing him in his chair along the esplanade when the weather allowed.

She had expected it to be for just a few months — a year at the most — for Mr Frobisher was old. The excitement of marriage, she had thought, when it came (as she knew it would) would hasten his end.

"You must be cared for, my dear," he told her, patting her hand. "You care for me so well."

When they were married he no longer paid her a salary. He was mean with money. She had discovered this in the nursing home and had known he would think of marriage because it would cost him less, though why he guarded his funds so carefully when he had no one to leave his fortune to was hard to explain. It was characteristic of the elderly rich, she had noticed before. Now she had to account for every penny she spent when shopping, and Matthew saw no reason to keep the woman who had come twice a week to do the cleaning.

As the months went by, Mrs Frobisher was instructed to practise still more thrift by frugal catering. He ordered her to serve mince, rice pudding, and custard instead of salmon, crème caramel, and fruit out of season. She began to adjust her housekeeping accounts to extract enough money for splurges in cafés when she was shopping. Then she would drink coffee or chocolate topped with rich cream and eat cakes and pastries before hurrying home to Matthew, who would be reading the *Financial Times*.

The doctor, who called regularly, praised her care of her elderly husband. He'd got rather difficult, Mrs Frobisher once confessed, but she knew it was simply his health that made him pernickety about details.

"A trust fund, my dear," Mr Frobisher had suddenly said one day. "You are not used to handling money. You'll be at the mercy of fortune hunters when I'm gone. I must protect you."

Mrs Frobisher was dismayed. She wanted her fortune, when she received it, to be her own, to handle as she desired. She had earned it, after all. She would travel. She planned to go on a cruise round the world, perhaps meet romance on a boat deck under the moon. She secretly read brochures picked up on her shopping trips, and daydreamed over them when Matthew slept. She was still only forty-six years old and she had never known love. A young man resembling a god, she romanced, might woo her in Greece. An Italian with deep brown eyes, perhaps, would serenade her in Venice.

While her husband slumbered, Mrs Frobisher escaped to a world of dreams. She read magazines, and romantic novels which she borrowed from the library without Mr Frobisher's knowledge. And she watched television, too, until late at night. She had formed an attachment in her mind to a handsome middle-aged actor who featured in many plays. He often played rather sinister roles and was suave. Mrs Frobisher, alone in her bed while Matthew snored nearby in his, would imagine the actor whispering to her, his lips on her neck, herself at last responding to physical passion, something that had eluded her in her life thus far.

Mr Frobisher, after their marriage, had requested intimate contact. He was capable only of touch, and that, he indicated, was his right now that they were husband and wife.

"It's not good for you, dear. You'll send up your blood pressure," Mrs Frobisher had said, avoiding compliance, promising it as a treat for one day in the future when he was better. But his hands, increasingly, reached for her as she dealt with his needs; he would watch her with narrowed eyes as she moved about their bedroom.

Mrs Frobisher had grown to hate her husband before he

threatened to curtail her future liberty by means of a trust and acted in time to prevent him.

It had been carefully planned.

At first she had thought of demanding money for personal spending, making him angry, and leaving his physical wants untended so that bedsores and other problems developed, but pride in her profession, finally, would not permit the use of these means to make his blood pressure rise and bring on another stroke — which he might have at any time. Though again, since his heart was strong, he might survive.

In the end, she had been more subtle. She had done it with frozen chicken, thawing it imperfectly and ceasing its cooking too soon, leaving it in the warm kitchen where it could begin to go off even if there were no risk of salmonella. It didn't work the first time, but the second attempt, when she'd made a chicken risotto and added lamb from the weekend joint which she had kept exposed until it started to smell rather nasty, did the trick.

She ate a little herself, so she could tell the doctor, truthfully, that she too had felt ill, but she disposed of all that was left down the lavatory, flushing it thoroughly.

He had lingered for twenty-four hours after the dreadful vomiting, his breathing harsh in the quiet room. She would not have him taken to the hospital. "I am a nurse," she said with pride.

For some hours she had feared he would recover again. She was tempted to lay a pillow over his face or pinch his nostrils, but suppose betraying signs resulted? She could wipe away any froth that might be exuded, but she couldn't disperse petechial haemorrhages if they occurred, and the doctor might observe them. He would look at his patient's eyes.

But such action was not needed.

Just before he died, Matthew opened his eyes and glared at her, seeing her clearly.

He knew. She and the doctor had discussed the possible cause of his food poisoning while Matthew lay there, and perhaps he had understood their conversation. He had known how careful she was in the kitchen, how unlikely the chance of contaminated food being served under her charge.

Well, he could do nothing now: it was too late. She stared back at him until it was over.

She had affected grief for a year, only slowly emerging in becoming, elegant clothes — in muted hues as first the executors advanced her funds and finally the estate, which was in perfect order, was settled. And tomorrow she was leaving on a world cruise. Her bags were packed and labelled. The porter in the block of flats knew of her plans. She had no intimate friends, but she told her few acquaintances that she was going away.

During her year of widowhood, Mrs Frobisher had put on weight, for she had made amends for the years of rice pudding and mince — but she could carry it off, she thought, regarding herself in the mirror. She had had her hair rinsed a rich honey blonde and had bought a mink coat. Her spectacles had been exchanged for contact lenses. She felt sure she would find romance on her voyage, though perhaps not of a durable kind. When she returned, she would open an expensive eventide home where rich elderly people could end their days in her experienced care and be off the hands of their families.

That evening, after her celebratory meal, a further treat awaited Mrs Frobisher — the perfect way to round off the day. The final instalment of a television-drama series in which her actor hero played a leading role. She had arranged her cruise for after the end of the series, not willing to miss any appearance he might make. And now, in this last episode, the chain of spellbinding events would be tied off.

Mrs Frobisher ate her smoked salmon with wafer-thin brown bread and butter. She had learned to cut it like that for her patients. She ate her succulent partridge, and to follow she had two chocolate éclairs bought at the new pâtisserie in town.

She piled the crockery into the dishwasher. She would turn it on in the morning after breakfast, before the taxi arrived to take her to the airport from which she was due to fly to join her cruise. She made coffee and poured out the last of the champagne to drink while she watched her play.

In the warm luxurious room, Mrs Frobisher sat in her deep armchair and gazed at the screen while her hero, captured by terrorists planning to kill him, sought to evade what seemed an inevitable fate. The camera cut to his wife (middle-aged and careworn) and his mistress (young and curvacious). The background was Spanish, the countryside burnt brown, baking in shimmering heat. Shots of a bullfight were briefly, irrelevantly, shown.

Mrs Frobisher's hero, bound and gagged, watched water entering his prison cell in the dungeon of an old castle. It lapped about his feet. The terrorists, on the ramparts, watched for the helicopter that would take them to safety.

The telephone rang in Mrs Frobisher's hall.

The sound startled her. She received few calls apart from an occasional message from the porter.

Could it be the shipping line? They had her number in case, as the booking clerk had explained, there were last-minute changes of plan, alterations to flights due to weather or other conditions.

She had better answer. She'd be quick, missing only moments of the play's approaching dénouement.

She brusquely gave her own number, and added "Mrs Frobisher speaking."

"Mavis — at last! I've had such a trouble to find you," a female voice said. "It's Beatrice. I've only just heard you'd got married. I'm so sorry to hear you've lost your husband."

"Beatrice!" Mrs Frobisher echoed.

"Yes. I traced you through the nursing agency," the voice of her younger sister declared.

Mrs Frobisher was too shocked to answer. From the living room came the sound of gunfire and the clattering noise of helicopter blades. Mrs Frobisher replaced the telephone receiver, ignoring the voice that continued to speak, and returned to the living room. She poured herself out a small brandy and was sipping it when the telephone started to ring again.

Mrs Frobisher sat watching the screen, letting it ring. The blood pounded in her temples. She had not heard from Beatrice for years. Her sister had married young and had four children — she lived in Wales with her farmer husband. What had happened to make Beatrice seek her out?

She wanted money, Mrs Frobisher thought. She must have discovered that Matthew had been a rich man.

Mrs Frobisher gazed at the screen, pouring a second brandy. While she was out of the room, her hero had somehow freed himself from his bonds and was now driving a car across a desert while shots were fired at him from a helicopter overhead.

The telephone went on ringing.

Mrs Frobisher rose, went into the hall, and took the receiver off the hook. Her hero, now wounded, was staggering on foot across a small river when she returned to her seat. On the far bank, his mistress was waiting, holding a chestnut horse by the bridle. The camera cut to the helicopter from which guns protruded.

Beatrice had always been a nuisance. She'd been cleverer than Mavis — and prettier, too, with boys hanging about her since she was fourteen. She'd got herself pregnant and had to get married, but hadn't seemed to mind the loss of her chances for betterment. Beatrice, who had not wanted one, had been assured of a university place, while Mavis, who sought advancement, had struggled to pass her nursing exams. She'd crossed swords more than once with ward sisters. Private nursing had been a haven, for she'd soon discovered which patients would pay with gifts for extra attention and which would accept good care as merely their right, so that it was not worth taking trouble for them.

Beatrice, getting in touch with her like this, must want something. It could only be money, for what else had Mavis that Beatrice might envy?

The hero, on her screen, struggled out of the river toward the outstretched hand of his mistress. Guns in the helicopter fired, and at that moment the screen flickered and went black.

It was not a power failure. The soft light from the table lamp beside Mrs Frobisher's chair burnt on. She rose and pressed various buttons on the set. She hit it and swore, but it remained dark.

The play had ten more minutes to run. Her hero was far from safe. She felt sure that in the end he would escape, but would his mistress survive, too, and how? Were the terrorists caught? The interruption, at such a tense time in the story, enraged Mrs

Frobisher. It was Beatrice's fault — if she hadn't telephoned, the set would not have gone wrong. All their lives, Beatrice had frustrated her sister and taken what was Mavis's due — her looks, her ability to do well at school, the attention, before he died, of their father. And now she had spoiled the perfection of Mrs Frobisher's special evening.

Mavis stood in front of the television set shaking her fists. Her face went red. The pounding continued inside her head.

As the picture, after a short break due to a transmitter fault, returned to her set, Mrs Frobisher was unable to see it, for she lay unconscious on the floor.

She lay there all night.

In the morning, the taxi that was to take her to the airport arrived. When the hall porter telephoned to tell her and there was no reply, he came up himself to knock at her door. In the end, he opened it with his master key.

Mrs Frobisher's blood pressure, never tested, had, unknown to her, long been high. She had eaten and drunk too well in her year as a widow, and rage and frustration had caused it to soar, bringing on a stroke.

Her eyes opened as she was lifted to a stretcher. She opened her mouth to speak, but no sound emerged. She tried to sit up, but she could not move.

Two days later, Beatrice came to the hospital where Mrs Frobisher, unable to ask for private attention, lay in a public ward. Though it was years since they had met, Mrs Frobisher recognised her at once, despite greying hair and a red weather-beaten complexion. There was that something about her — an aura. Mrs Frobisher knew the word as she stared at the hated face. It was joy. Beatrice was a happy woman.

"Poor Mavis. How terribly sad," Beatrice said, taking Mrs Frobisher's unresponsive hand which lay neatly on top of the sheet, convenient for the nurse who would take her pulse. "No wonder you couldn't answer the telephone after we were cut off. If only I'd realised, you'd have been found much sooner. Fancy the television still on in the morning, making a terrible noise. But don't worry: I'll see that you're taken care of. I was trying to find you to tell you that Hugh — my eldest son — that his wife has had twins. You're a great-aunt, Mavis. Isn't that nice?" She squeezed Mavis's hand. "I'm sure you can understand what I'm saying," her voice went on. "We've been out of touch too long. Families should stick together. You were hard to trace. You've moved about a lot since you did your training."

Mavis's eyes looked up at the ceiling. She heard and understood every word, but she could not reply.

"Still, you're not short of money, are you? The doctor thinks you have a good chance of getting much better, but you'll always need looking after. I'll take you home with me when you can travel." Again Beatrice patted the motionless hand. "I'm your next-of-kin, after all."

THE ELIXIR

Glyn Hardwicke

There we sat, Henry Tremayne and I, one on each side of my brother's bed, watching him die.

It was a curious situation, made more curious by the extraordinary environment in which my brother had chosen to live. A great, insensitive bullock of a man, he had for some inexplicable reason settled on a Victorian winter as the setting he most enjoyed. And it was really quite difficult to believe, as he lay in his final coma, that in the world outside the bedroom which the heavy curtains totally excluded, it was a sunny afternoon in the summer of 1973.

The walls were of dark oak panelling from floor to ceiling, the curtains of plum-coloured velvet which blended darkly with the deep red thick pile carpet. The bed on which he lay was a four-poster with a canopy of dark green which was duplicated in the bedspread. Between the floor-length windows which the curtains shrouded stood one of those ancient marble-topped wash-stands, bearing a large porcelain basin and jug, as if the running water in the rest of the house had not yet been installed. On the opposite wall a heavy desk — in mahogany, which clashed with the panelling — held a typewriter not merely old but antique, and a number of small but heavy gilt frames each holding an early photograph which may have had nothing at all to do with our family, though they could not be distinguished in the near darkness of the room. The wall at the foot of the bed was dominated by a huge Victorian wardrobe, five or six feet wide, which rose almost to the ceiling. The atmosphere was unpleasantly oppressive, and our discomfort, had he been conscious, would have added materially to the sadistic pleasure of the obese hulk whom we had been summoned to see breathing his last.

Periodically, noticing a few small beads of sweat on the dying man's brow, Tremayne leaned forward and wiped it with a napkin damped with a solution of water and *eau de cologne*, the faint perfume of which served temporarily to hide the sickly scent of approaching death.

I had always felt sorry for Tremayne, knowing how the loyalty with which he was imbued was so often in bilious conflict with the deep sensitivity which was his core. It was far easier for me, for I had trained myself for most of my life to block out, mentally and physically, the unpleasantness which had clung from childhood to the persona of my brother.

Technically we were not brothers but half-brothers. The mother we shared had been one of those frail-seeming Grecian women who constantly surprised everyone by surviving the strong ones around them. Her first husband, my brother's father, a bullying monster like his son, broke his neck in a riding accident. Her second, my father, a modest man with a fortune that was anything but modest, had died of pneumonia when I was only four. Having survived both of them, the mother we shared died in her nineties as placidly as she had lived.

By then, of course, both my brother and I had long since come to England and changed our names. Mikhail Stratos, as he was born, had taken on the cloak of Michael Strathy, and acquired an international reputation as a gourmet and authority on wine, which he deployed with such consummate skill that very few people knew it to be quite phoney. I for my part, having started life as Claudius Paragionis, had become Claude Paragon — my adopted surname being the product not, as some may have thought, of arrogance but of enchantment, since I took it from the name of a street in the lovely Georgian city of Bath where I found a kind acceptance and eventually appreciable wealth as an antique dealer. Between us there had always existed not mere sibling rivalry but active dislike. Michael had bullied the daylights out of me as a child. It may have been the regular beatings he inflicted on me that gave him the taste for violence he had since always enjoyed. If so, then they did him more harm than me, whom they provided only with the stimulus to be as unlike him as I could.

Suddenly on the giant bed my brother's body moved. Ever since my arrival he had lain inert, unresponsive to the tender ministrations of Tremayne. I had assumed that this would continue until he died. But now he stirred, as if recoiling from Tremayne's perfunctory dabbing with the napkin. Doubtless it was simply the body making itself more comfortable, unconnected with any brain activity, but for a moment I thought he was about to open his eyes and return to full consciousness, looking with the old contempt upon both of us, before raking Tremayne with some unnecessarily offensive criticism. A moment of fear, a reflex conditioned by recollections of childhood, bubbled up through the years of patiently acquired insulation. I glanced across the bed and thought I saw a not dissimilar reaction flit across the face of my companion.

"The doctor did say he was coming back?" I asked.

"Oh yes, quite definitely. He's got this emergency nearby — the next block of flats, I believe. I gather his patient there is in a high fever approaching a crisis and it's important that he should be present. But he knows Michael's state exactly. He promised to be back again before the end."

"I hope he's in time."

"He seemed quite confident. I asked him if there was anything we could do,but he said there was nothing. It's just a question of watching and waiting, I'm afraid."

"There's no chance of Michael coming out of the coma?"

"None at all. The doctor was clear. He may move very slightly, like he did just then, but it's really just the body gradually letting go — giving up."

"Something that Michael was always reluctant to do," I said with a wry smile which I didn't expect to be returned — and wasn't.

Henry Tremayne and I had been fellow pupils at Marlborough in the middle 1930s, when we had become good friends. If some form of "collective memory" had contributed to my expertise in the old languages, Tremayne was a genuine natural linguist, with an ear which could embrace not merely the vocabulary, the grammar and the "sound" of a language but the idioms and nuances which make each tongue a living thing.

We had both left school shortly before the outbreak of the Second World War and had met again, to our joint pleasure, in the Intelligence Corps. My early upbringing had given good reason for the army to keep Greece on my records and, after a spell as a general interrogator of German prisoners, I was sent to my native land, to carry out certain duties about which I do not nowadays choose to talk. But when I landed one dark night in a small bay in the Peloponnese, it was a relief and a delight to be greeted by Henry Tremayne, and we were together, on and off, throughout the rest of the war.

Back in England in peacetime, Henry learned of my relationship to Michael and sought an introduction. Naturally I was at a loss to understand why one so worthwhile should be anxious to make the acquaintance of someone who seemed to me to be diametrically opposite in character to himself. On the other hand, Henry was a friend whom I had come to value most highly — indeed, he had twice literally saved my life — and I did not hesitate. What my coarse brother had ever done to attract the adulation of as gentle a soul as Tremayne I never knew, but I felt that even so insensitive a brute as Michael could not fail eventually to respond to such obvious appreciation, and few men can long resist genuine and unceasing admiration.

Michael was by this time famous as a *bon vivant*, and I equipped Tremayne with a letter of introduction and followed it up with a phone call to Michael which, as usual, turned my stomach. And some months later, I was pleased to receive a warm letter from Tremayne saying that he had become my brother's amanuensis and personal assistant. What Michael paid him I have no idea — he could certainly afford to be generous. I saw Tremayne only occasionally but gathered he was content in the position.

Then one weekend he contacted me, saying that he had some kind of "mission" in the West Country and suggesting it could be combined with a reunion. He arrived in Bath, I remember, one Friday evening. After dinner in my flat, he said only that his visit concerned a very rare item in the gastronomic world. I was naturally curious, but though I rather expected him to enlarge on the topic, he seemed politely secretive and, having no motive beyond curiosity, I did not press him. We spent a quiet but happy evening, reminiscing about adventures shared during the war, and I put him up for the night.

He was off in a hired car early the next morning and I did not see him again for some years. Then I had a letter from him, warning me that Michael had suffered a kidney failure and was not expected to last more than a day or two. The letter seemed unusually formal — I forget exactly what he said, but in its mood it was not unlike that celebrated bulletin posted on the railings of Buckingham Palace in January 1936 about the dying George V — "The King's life is moving peacefully to its close." Apparently Michael had evinced a strong desire that I should be present at the end and, despite misgivings, I felt obligated. Which is how Henry and I came to be sitting on either side of Michael's bed, watching him die.

Now I noticed that Michael's breathing had started to become shallower. I looked across at Tremayne, wondering what if anything we should do, and at that moment the door bell rang and he went quickly to answer it, bringing the doctor — a bright young man named Lister — back with him, stethoscope already in hand. With a nod to me, he listened to Michael's chest and then said quietly, "It's a matter of minutes, I'm afraid. He's in a coma, you understand. He has no idea what's happening to him. I'll stay until he's gone, and then I must dash off again, if you'll excuse me."

So the moment was approaching. I got up out of my chair — I really don't know why but it seemed the right thing to do, somehow. Tremayne did the same on his side of the bed. And as we stood there, Michael again stirred slightly, as if to make himself more comfortable, and there was a little sound, something like a tiny gurgle, in his throat. The doctor nodded, stepped forward and again listened with his stethoscope. Then he just smiled sadly and said "That's it, I'm afraid." Tremayne stood motionless for a moment with bowed head, and I did more or less the same. Michael's face looked very peaceful and, for the first time in my recollection, quite gentle. There was actually a suggestion of a smile on his face. The doctor covered him with the sheet and then left us, as arranged, saying he would return as soon as he could, to complete the death certificate and so forth. Henry showed him to the door and came back. And then a number of things happened.

Tremayne suddenly took a deep breath and reached out, flicked the sheet back from the dead man's face and stood looking down at him for a few seconds. A look of intense distaste came over his face.

"Ah well — that's that, then, Claude." He looked up and stared at me in a strange way. "Or is it?" he added.

"What do you mean, Henry?"

"Have you wondered why Michael should have been so anxious that you should be here with me to watch him die?" he said with a quizzical smile.

"Not really. I just assumed that a dying man might prefer to be with his friends and family rather than alone."

"Oh, there was a better reason than that, Claude. A very good reason. You are to be a witness."

"A witness to what?"

Again that curious smile. "You heard the doctor pronounce him dead, didn't you?"

I nodded. Tremayne bent down beside the bed on his side and came back up holding a briefcase which must have been at his feet. From it with care he took a little half-litre bottle with a sherry-type cork in it. This he placed carefully on the bedside table.

"Know what's in that, Claude?" he smiled.

I shook my head, quite mystified.

"It is just a drop — a little drop — of something so rare and precious that few people have ever seen it, let alone tasted it."

I sank into my chair, my eyes on my friend's face. Then something flickered in the back of my memory. "Is it a wine? Or possibly a liqueur?" I asked.

"It is neither, Claude."

"Some form of non-alcoholic tisane?"

"No, it is alcoholic all right, though only about fourteen degrees, which is less than sherry and very little more than many table wines. It has been described as the attar — the very quintessence — of the grape. It is the legendary Tokaji Aszu

Essencia. The description of it that I like best is that coined, or
perhaps stolen, by Michael himself - 'To drink it is as if one were
penetrating gradually into the heart of the grape, discovering the
true nectar that men have always believed lay there.' It has even
been proclaimed as the elixir of life itself."

"I have heard of it, vaguely," I said. "It comes from Hungary,
doesn't it?"

"It does indeed. From the hills of north-eastern Hungary. In a
sense, it is a unique extension of that country's rarest and
greatest wine, the celebrated Tokaji Aszu, which is an unfort-
ified wine made from individually picked grapes suffering from
what the French call *pourriture noble*. Essencia itself dates back
to 1650. It is probably the rarest drink in the world. Even Aszu is
made only in exceptional years when the summer has been
perfect. And compared to Essencia, Aszu is almost common!"

"Ah — it's coming back to me now. Isn't this the liquid for
which the grapes are never pressed — they're just allowed to
bleed under their own weight?"

"Exactly. Little drips from those shrivelled, rotten grapes are
collected in stone jars. When there is no more to drip, what
remains of the grapes is reduced to a mash of pulp, skin and pips
which is mixed with an exceptional Szamorodni wine. What
results is identified by the number of *puttonyos* — hodfuls —
which are added. Then they're taken in casks called *gonci* down
into the cellars where they go through not one or two but a whole
series of tiny fermentations over the next six or seven years.
Eventually the liquid clarifies itself and is allowed to mature in
partly filled casks with loosely fitting bungs. A thick layer of
blue-black fungus forms everywhere during this process, which
feeds on the bacteria in the wine and helps to mature it further."

"And what you've got is Essencia, is it?" I asked.

"Oh no, my dear Claude — all this is to achieve the great
Tokaji Aszu. Essencia is a whole stage beyond that again. It can
be made only when there is enough Aszu wine of the highest
quality. Even then it sometimes 'doesn't take', and the whole
production is lost. The last year in which any was made was in
1964, the last before that was in 1934 and it may be decades
before the conditions allow more. Some people think they can

deduce how it is made, but it has never been explained fully, and there are parts of the process which remain a complete mystery to everyone."

"And yet here is some in England, of all places!"

He eyed me steadily. "This is the last known drop of the legendary 1934. It is said to be the longest-lived drink in the world — quite unaffected by oxydisation, for some mysterious reason. And that is only part of the magical properties attributed to it. Only one English firm has ever been allowed by the Hungarian government to import any — Berry Brothers and Rudd, of St James's. Last autumn, they obtained a small consignment of the 1964, the first Essencia for thirty years. It was offered to a handful of their most favoured customers."

"And you were among them?"

"No. Do you remember the evening a few years ago when I came down and spent a night with you in Bath?"

I nodded. "Vividly. You said something about a special mission and I didn't like to ask what it was."

"I knew you were not the type to question an old friend about something he wanted not to talk about. Well, I had heard, purely by chance, that there was an old man in the country not far from Bath who was understood to own a bottle of the 1934."

"Good Lord!"

"I tracked him down and called there. Of course so few people know anything about Essencia that it is often not recognised what it might be worth. Nor is that the only mystery about it. Its effects, too, are legendary, you know."

"Yes — didn't someone administer it to a very elderly aunt who was simply fading away, and it revived her completely?"

"Oh, that's a very well authenticated incident. But it's not unique by any means. At one time, Berrys kept a list with details of dozens of documented cases where their customers had effected cures by means of Essencia varying from the dramatic to the sensational."

"And you bought this bottle?" He nodded. "You were on a mission for Michael?"

"It rather depends what you mean by that! If you mean that Michael had sent me, you are wrong. He had no idea that the old man existed. But it was for Michael in the sense that I intended to give it to him on his seventieth birthday, last March."

"It was a present for him about which he knew nothing, you mean?"

"Just so."

"What a gift! I hope he appreciated it!"

He sighed and glanced towards the corpse.

"Well, you know how completely I admired your brother, Claude — how I had done for many years. It was thanks to you that I was able to meet him in the first place. He had been my ultimate hero ever since boyhood."

"To be candid, Henry, I have never been able to understand why."

"I know. You regarded me as a reasonably sensitive soul, and Michael as the reverse. Basically, you were right. Over the years I spent with him, there were many occasions on which he not only treated me like dirt — he enjoyed doing so. It was as if he was so sure nothing would shake my admiration for him that he wanted to see to what lengths he could go. The strange thing was, however, that his repeated insults became for me a constant challenge. I guess it was sheer bloody obstinacy. I was determined that *nothing* he could do would break my willingness to stick with him. Not that he was always like that, of course. There were times when he was so kind, I could have wept. But they became fewer and further between. Eventually something had to bring this absurd situation to a head. And it was the Essencia."

"You gave it to him? On his birthday?"

"I did. At first he had no idea what it was. I explained how I had got hold of it. For several minutes he sat staring at the little bottle. And then he looked at me. The gratitude he could not escape feeling was slowly replaced by the realisation that this was the ultimate test of how far I would go without breaking. He just said 'Bring a glass, Henry.' I went over to the sideboard, collected two ordinary goblets, and put them on the table in front of him. He opened the bottle and poured some into one of the glasses. Slowly he picked it up, held it to the light, then nosed it. He was almost trembling with excitement. He had told me more than once that this was about the only gastronomic experience he had never undergone. And then he drank it. Not sipped it — drank it. A wine glass full. And then he picked up the bottle and poured himself another. And then a third. I simply stood at the other end of the dining-table, watching him. He never took his eyes off me. Glass by glass he sat there drinking. And then he held up the bottle to the light and said 'There's just a little drop left, Henry. We'll cork that up very tightly. We shall keep it until the time comes for me to die. And when I have been pronounced dead, and not before, you will pour that last little drop into my mouth. And *then* we shall see whether Essencia is all they say about it — whether it really is the elixir of life!'"

I shook my head and regarded the face of my dead brother. The smile on his lips seemed more cynical now, somehow.

"And he never gave you so much as a taste of it?"

"Not a sniff. Mind — I think that before the end I had determined that if he had poured some for me, I would have thrown it straight in his face. For I *had* cracked, Claude. My devotion had turned suddenly and at last to hatred. But I knew that I must not show it. Somehow I had to convince him that he had failed yet again to make me hate him — failed even with what he thought was the ultimate weapon. If he never knew I had lost, he would think that I had won. And he never did know. He never knew that he had taken his sadistic pitcher once too often to the well of my toleration. So I had won, after all!"

There was an interval of silence.

"And what are you going to do now, Henry?"

"I'm going to carry out his last wishes, Claude. In your presence — just as he directed me. Watch carefully, now!"

From the small table beside the bed he took a spoon and, opening the bottle, he poured the Essencia from the bottle into it. Then he put the bottle down and opened the dead man's lips. Slowly, he poured the liquid, drop by drop, on to the dead man's front teeth. After a moment or two, it filtered into Michael's mouth. He waited until it had all gone and turned to me and laughed. A vicious, cruel laugh. And then from his waistcoat pocket he took a little fob watch, and looked at it.

"Ten minutes. That'll teach him!"

"Teach him what, Henry?"

"You see, my dear Claude — I have carried out Michael's wish to the letter. But he neglected to tell me to do it within the first four minutes after clinical death."

"Why have you told me all this?" asked Charles Stratton.

"My dear Charles," I answered, "you're not only my solicitor — you're a true friend. Besides — it's troubled me far too long. I simply had to get it off my chest."

Stratton thought for a moment. Then he smiled.

"Well, the problem is nothing like as serious as you seem to imagine, Claude. Tremayne is in the clear."

"In the clear?"

"Yes. It isn't murder to refrain from trying to revive someone who has been pronounced medically dead by a qualified doctor."

I understood what he was saying, but I was rendered speechless by it. Twice I tried to start speaking but stopped before a single comprehensible word emerged. The third time, I found my voice.

"But — the Essencia. . . ."

"If your brother Michael had come back to life, you mean? Again — legally, no problem. Even the best of doctors make occasional honest mistakes. There are lots of authenticated cases of people who have been pronounced dead, waking up on the mortuary slab, being revived, and walking around quite normally today. All that would have happened is that the death certificate would have been cancelled — withdrawn — as if it had never been made out."

Suddenly, passionately, I regained my fluency.

"But don't you see, Charles? Tremayne meant him to come back as a vegetable! That was going to be his revenge for how my brother had treated him over all those years!"

"Oh, I see that, of course" said Stratton in his measured way. "But the law on murder is concerned with the continuance of life, not the quality of it. If your little miracle had in fact happened, Tremayne would still not have been guilty of any criminal offence, I assure you."

For a long time, I sat staring blankly at my solicitor and friend. Finally I said in a tone that conveyed my anguish, "You have misunderstood me, my dear Charles. I have never been in the slightest concerned with Tremayne's legal guilt or innocence. You have just convicted me of murder."

He stared at me. "You, Claude? Murder? But how?"

"By suffocation. On that dreadful afternoon, after Tremayne administered the elixir and told me the nature of his revenge, I was appalled. Before Tremayne could stop me, I jumped forward and lay across Michael's head — his face. It was all over in a second or two. It was I who murdered my own brother!"

"But he was already dead, man!"

"Dead, you say? Can you imagine what a creature — alive but without a brain — is like? Charles — I felt him shudder underneath me. I simply couldn't let it go on!"

For a long moment there was complete silence in the room. And then Stratton's hand went to his mouth.

"Oh God! Claude — you don't mean — it worked. . . ?"

THE LAST TENANT

Michael Gilbert

Fred Jury and Johnny Tredgett would have described themselves, if they had thought of the word, as seasonal workers.
They were prepared to tackle any job which called for muscle
rather than brain power. Sorting and humping packages at the
Crossways Goods Depot was their favourite occupation for the
cold wet months of winter and early spring. With the turn of the
year they liked to be out and about. They were not skilled
enough to tackle the more sophisticated building trades but there
was always rough work to be done; demolition, rubble shifting,
drain laying and foundation digging. The local foremen knew
them for good workers, with the bonus of a head for heights.
They were seldom out of a job for long.

On this lovely April morning they were perched on a remnant
of brick wall, sixty feet above the pavement, demolishing what
had once been a snug little turret room at the top of a block of
offices at the corner of Endless Street and Barton Street.

All that was left of the inner wall of the room was a fireplace
with an imitation marble mantelshelf painted dark green and a
mirror set in the wall above it. The three outer walls had already
been demolished.

"Be a bit careful with that," said Fred. "Personally, I could use
it myself. Go nicely in the front room."

Johnny slid the point of his pick into the plaster beside the
mirror. A lump came away but there was solid brickwork behind
the plaster.

"Odd old way to fix a mirror," he said. He probed again. More
plaster fell. The glass remained immovable.

He said, "If we can't shift her we'd better bust her, right?
Don't want to be all day about it."

"Of course," said Fred. "Naturally, if you're looking for seven years bad luck, go ahead and bust it. Don't mind me. Just go right ahead. Bust it."

"That's a lot of bullshit," said Johnny, but he lowered his pick.

"My Uncle Arthur smashed a big looking-glass. Just after the war. Nothing went right for him after that. First his brother died. Then he got into trouble with the National Insurance for trying to steam the stamps off his brother's card and stick them on to his own. Then he got piles."

Fred, who had started scratching away at the other side of the mirror, said, "Take a look at that, will you."

The glass, it was now clear, was set in an iron frame. It was clear, too, why they had been unable to shift it. The frame was hinged to a metal upright which was itself set in the brickwork. He said, "It's a sort of cupboard door really. The catch must be on your side."

Some more careful work with the point of the pick and the secret of the mirror was revealed. A small square of wood, painted the same colour as the plaster, came away. Under it was a keyhole in the iron frame.

"All we've got to do," said Johnny, "is get those bricks loose. We won't have no more trouble then." It took ten minutes to loosen the bricks all round the frame. Then they started to lever it out. As they did so, the foreman, who had climbed up behind them, said, "What are you two layabouts playing at? You ought to have had the whole wall down by now. God Almighty!"

He was staring at something Fred had picked out of the brick-lined cavity behind the looking-glass door.

Detective Chief Inspector Patrick Petrella was walking to work. It was exactly a mile from his new flat to Patton Street Police Station and in fine weather the walk made a good start to a day most of which had to be spent inside his office. He was humming to himself as he walked. It wasn't just the weather. The wheels of existence seemed, for once, to be turning smoothly. There were encouraging reports on the progress of young-Petrella-to-be. A girl, this time, he felt sure. The rougher elements in his manor seemed to have declared an armistice for the moment. There was enough petty crime to keep them all from getting bored, but nothing which called for lengthy reports to Division or District. He had no reason to suppose that this happy state of affairs would last, but his years in the police service had taught him to live in the present.

In the charge room three men were awaiting his arrival, under the eye of Station Sergeant Cove. Two were tough cheerful youngsters in their working clothes. The third was an older man, a foreman, he guessed. Stacked on the counter was a pile of cardboard boxes.

"Thought you might like to look at this little collection," said Sergeant Cove. "These boys just brought it along."

The largest of the boxes, an open shoe box, was crammed with banknotes, ones and fives in bundles.

"Haven't counted them yet," said Sergeant Cove. "But there must be more'n a thousand nicker there, wouldn't you say."

"A lot more than that, I should guess," said Petrella. He eased one of the bundles of fivers out of the box. They were packed so tightly that it was a job to get them out. There were forty notes in that bundle. Fred and Johnny watched him hungrily.

"Two hundred here. Must be three or four thousand altogether. What's in the other boxes?"

"Valuables," said Fred.

"Joolery," said Johnny.

It was good run-of-the-mill stuff. Gold chains and knick-knacks. Rings set with small diamonds and rubies. Wrist watches. Gold pens and pencils. Lighters, cigar cutters. Everything looked new and unused. There was a necklace made out of linked gold coins that Petrella seemed to remember.

He said to the foreman, "We'll have to check these things in our lists. I've got a feeling that necklace is part of the stuff that was lifted from Adamsons last month. You did quite right to bring it along. We'll list it and give you a receipt."

The foreman said, "If any of it should be unclaimed, it was these boys who found it. They were knocking down the back wall of the very top room — "

"Easier to show me than talk about it," said Petrella. "Come on." The truth was he was glad of an excuse to get out into the sunshine again.

Ten minutes later he was wondering if he had been sensible. He had a fair head for heights. The real trouble was that there was nothing to hold on to.

"Easier if you sit down," said the foreman sympathetically.

"How on earth do you *work* up here?" said Petrella.

"Nothing to it, once you get used to it," said Johnny, balancing on a narrow ledge of brickwork and holding his pick in one hand.

After a minute Petrella felt better. He hauled himself up on to his feet, edged forward and peered into the cavity over the fireplace.

"How do you suppose it worked?" he said.

"Small square of wood," said Fred. "Fitted into the plaster, over the lock. Pick it out and undo the lock, always supposing you had the key. Then the mirror swings open."

It was a neat job and the steelwork looked new. Petrella said, "Who had this office, anyway?"

The foreman scratched his head and consulted his memory. "This'd be the turret room, wouldn't it? Fifth floor. Leo Hinn. Called himself an export agent."

"I wonder what he exported," said Petrella.

Later that morning he asked the same question of Mr Tasker, the solicitor at the Oval.

Mr Tasker said he thought it might have been hides or furs or something of that sort. Hinn wasn't a regular client. He'd arranged the letting for him about two years ago. After some searching he found a thin folder of papers. There were two short hand-written notes on flimsy writing paper, with no address at the top and signed with a sort of hieroglyphic seeming to be made up of the letters L and H.

"He always signed his letters like that," said Mr Tasker. "I had the devil of a job finding out where he lived. I finally tracked him down to a room he rents from a Mrs Tappin in Pardoe Street, Number 46."

"Did he have a lease?"

"Of the office you mean? Certainly not. If you have a lease, you pay stamp duty. He was quite happy with a letter from the landlords telling him he could have the room and what rent he had to pay. I initialled it on his behalf."

"Who are the landlords?"

"At that time it was Fullbrights. A very decent old outfit. When Charlie Fullbright died last year they sold out to Lempard. Rather different sort of type."

"Different?"

"I don't mean bent. An eye to the main chance. All Lempard ever wanted with this particular building was to knock it down. Can't blame him really. Shockingly designed. Full of big hallways and corridors and a lot of air space taken up with turrets and battlements. He reckoned they could put up a modern building on the site with twice the lettable area. Offices on top, shops underneath."

"If he wanted to pull it down, I suppose he had to get rid of the tenants first?"

"That's right," said Mr Tasker. "That's just what he did. He got rid of the tenants. It's a technique. You start by buying out the ground-floor tenant. You don't re-let. You just allow the ground-floor office to deteriorate. Maybe you board up the windows. The other tenants get a bit edgy. Perhaps another one pulls out. That gives you an excuse to lock up the main entrance. If there are only three or four tenants left, well, they can use the side entrance. Then the lift goes wrong. Of course, they're going to repair it, but it takes time. So the old gent who has the office on the third floor has to climb the stairs three or four times a day. It's surprising how quickly people take the hint."

"I see," said Petrella. It sounded dirty, but not quite criminal. "And he got them all out."

"He thought he had. Somehow he'd overlooked little Mr Hinn, tucked away in his turret room. He was easy to overlook. Five foot nothing and no weight at all. As I was saying, Sam Lempard forgot about him. He made all his arrangements to pull the place down, signed up the builders, borrowed the money and was ready to press the button when someone said, 'Hold on a moment. What about old Hinn? Can't start work whilst he's there.' Talk about a row! He sacked his lawyers. Mellors and Rapp were acting for him at the time. Made out it was their fault, which was a load of nonsense. Then he tried to bully little Mr Hinn. He wouldn't be bullied. Then he tried to buy him and he wouldn't be bought. Next he served a notice of dilapidation on him. There are agents who specialise in that sort of thing."

He mentioned a name and Petrella nodded. He knew them well.

"That was when Mr Hinn came to me. I told him to ignore the notice. Tear it up. No court would enforce it. Not with the building in that state and going to be pulled down anyway. He didn't only tear up the notice. Dear me, no. He served a counter-notice on Sam Lempard, under the Landlord and Tenant Act, asking for a new tenancy. Ha! I enjoyed doing that for him."

"You say Lempard sacked Mellors. Who was acting for him?"

Mr Tasker made a face and said, "Eric Duxford, who else?"

"Who else," agreed Petrella.

"He was in a corner. What with lay-off payments to the builders and interest on the money they'd borrowed the delay must have been costing him a thousand a week and old man Hinn could have hung him up for three months, no question. Once the court heard the whole story — which I should have been delighted to tell them — he might even have got a new lease."

"So what did Lempard do?"

"I guess he did the only thing he could. Offered Hinn a really large sum of money. Too big for him to refuse."

"You *guess* that's what happened. But you don't know?"

"I don't know, because that's the last I saw of Mr Hinn. He cleared out altogether. If you do find him, you might remind him that he hasn't paid my bill yet."

"When I find Mr Hinn," said Petrella, "I shall have quite a lot of questions to ask him."

Samuel Lempard described himself as a property consultant. He had a handsome set of offices in Kentledge Road with a convenient rear exit into Kentledge Mews, where he kept one of his three cars. This enabled him to dodge importunate or indignant clients. He seemed unsurprised to receive a visit from Detective Chief Inspector Petrella. Word of what had happened on his building site that morning must already have reached him. He said, "It's a queer do. What do you make of it, Inspector?"

"It's a bit early to be certain," said Petrella. "We haven't had time to check out all the stuff yet. One bit, at least, is on the 'Recently Stolen List'. If it all turns out to be stolen goods, we shall have to assume that Mr Hinn didn't confine his activities to dealing in hides and furs."

"A fence, eh?" said Mr Lempard. "It doesn't surprise me a lot. He was a shifty little bastard."

"And took a bit of shifting," said Petrella.

Mr Lempard's face showed a mottled red and Petrella could see the veins in his neck swelling. He said to himself, "By God, he *has* got a temper. He can't think of it, even now, without coming to the boil." The flush subsided slowly. As soon as Mr Lempard could speak he grunted out, "So you heard about that, eh?"

"I heard about it. And I want to hear more about it."

"Where the hell do the police come into my business?" He was still angry.

"Not your business. Mr Hinn's business."

Sam Lempard thought about it. Petrella imagined he could read his thoughts. Was there anything in it for him? He'd paid out good money to little Mr Hinn. There'd been a boxful of notes in the cache behind the mirror. A lot of it was probably his money. Was this a chance to get some of it back?

In the end he said, "I don't see why I shouldn't tell you. You heard how he stuck me up. Straight blackmail. Prompted by Geoff Tasker, I don't doubt. In the end I paid him two thousand quid, in notes, and he signed the necessary document."

"A surrender of his lease."

"That's right. Duxford drew it up. Hinn came round here the same evening and signed it."

"What happened then?"

Mr Lempard looked surprised. He said, "I don't follow you. He got out, of course."

"But what happened exactly? Did he clear all his stuff out and hand over the keys?"

"Now you come to mention it, that was a bit funny. Duxford and I went round the next morning. We found the door locked."

"So?"

"We broke it down."

"Wasn't that a bit irregular?"

"I don't see it. We'd paid the money. We could do what we liked with the place."

"And the furniture?"

"There were a few sticks there. Not what I'd call furniture." Mr Lempard looked round complacently at his own massively furnished office. "A desk, two or three chairs, a bookcase with a few trade catalogues in it."

"What did you do with it?"

"We sold it. No point in paying storage charges."

The scholarly Sergeant Ambrose said, "We've placed all the stuff. It's the proceeds of three shop-breakings. We had the proprietors round here with their records and they were able to identify every piece. Adamsons, in the High Street, Alpha Jewellery Sales in the Cut, and Hingstons. All the watches and pens came from Hingstons."

"You mean we've got it all back?"

"No such luck. About a quarter of Hingstons and a third of the other two."

Petrella thought about it. It was beginning to add up. He said, "The M.O. people tipped Mick the Pat for all those jobs, didn't they?"

"I have the relevant report here," said Sergeant Ambrose. He could always produce the relevant report. Petrella wondered what they were going to do when Sergeant Ambrose was promoted, as inevitably he would be, and removed to an office desk at New Scotland Yard. "It was a definite identification. Method of entry. Timing. Method of neutralising the alarms."

Petrella grunted. The *modus operandi* files were useful at pointing the finger of suspicion. They were never conclusive enough to justify an arrest. He said, "Irish Mick's a violent character. But I wouldn't have thought he went in for murder."

"Do you think Hinn's dead, then?" said Sergeant Blencowe, who had been listening to the conversation.

"It must be a strong possibility. The first idea was that he'd scarpered. That doesn't hold up. He was fencing Mick's stuff for him. That's clear. If he'd got cold feet and decided to scarper, he might have left the rest of the stuff behind, but he'd surely have taken the money."

"Unless he had to get out so quick he couldn't reach the money. If Mick thought he was being short-changed he'd have been after him with a pick helve."

"For God's sake!" said Petrella. "The money wasn't buried six feet down in the middle of a blasted heath. He'd only got to open his patent looking-glass cupboard and put the stuff in his pockets. I think we'll call on his last known address. You can come with me, Sergeant."

Pardoe Street was composed of small semi-detached houses which had been undistinguished when they were built and were now sliding into slumdom. The door of Number 46 was opened to them by a thin woman wearing an overall and carrying four empty milk bottles impaled on the fingers of her left hand. Mrs Tappin, Petrella guessed.

He introduced himself and said, "I believe Mr Hinn had rooms here. I suppose he isn't in just now?"

"Haven't seen him for more'n a month," said Mrs Tappin. As she spoke she clanked the milk bottles on her fingers like castanets. Sergeant Blencowe watched her, fascinated.

"I suppose you've re-let the room."

"Can't do that. Paid up three months." Clank, clank —

"Then no one's been in it for a month."

"Just his friends."

"Which friends?"

"Two men. Big men." Mrs Tappin demonstrated their size with a rattle on her castanets.

"I think we'd better have a look round."

"I expect that's right," said the woman. She deposited the milk bottles expertly on the top step. "After all, it's more'n a month. He might be anywhere by now, mightn't he?"

"He might indeed," said Petrella.

Mrs Tappin led the way up three narrow flights of stairs. The first flight had a carpet on it, the second linoleum, the third nothing at all. She extracted a key from the mysteries of her upper garments and unlocked the door on the left of the landing and opened it. They all looked in.

"His friends seem to have been untidy sort of people," said Petrella mildly.

The place was in chaos. Drawers pulled out, furniture overturned, the carpet rolled back, books tipped out of shelves, pictures wrenched from their frames.

"Well, now," said Mrs Tappin, "why would they want to do that?" She didn't seem unduly surprised. A life spent letting rooms in Pardoe Street must have made her a difficult person to surprise. She picked up one of the chairs and stood it carefully on its feet. "I expect they were looking for something."

"I guess they were," said Petrella. He took a photograph out of his wallet. "Would that have been one of the men?"

"Could have been," said Mrs Tappin. "I didn't notice him all that clearly."

"Had he got an Irish accent?"

"He might have had. I wouldn't want to swear to it in court."

"She recognised him all right," said Sergeant Blencowe. They were back at Patton Street. "She didn't want to say so, in case Mick came back and duffed her up. What a character! I must try it when I get home."

"Try what?"

"Playing tunes with milk bottles. Amuse the kids."

"You're not going to have much time for playing with your kids in the near future," said Petrella. "You're going to do a check-up on Mr Hinn. Former places of work, family, pubs and eating places he used. Have a word with the Social Security. And try the Russian Orthodox Church down in Little Baltic. It's a long shot but Tasker said his family originally came from Lithuania or some place like that. You know the form."

Sergeant Blencowe agreed, gloomily, that he knew the form. It was not that he objected to hard work. But he knew Little Baltic, a huddle of factories, slaughter houses and skinning shops which stank even in cool weather and were full of men who jabbered in their own God-forgotten lingo.

The next thing that happened was the arrival at Patton Street of Irish Mick. Petrella had had dealings with him before and had once described him as honestly dishonest. He was a huge man (by Mrs Tappin's units of measurement ten milk bottles in height and eight round the waist). He maintained a large family by his efforts at shop-breaking, being, for all his bulk, remarkably clever with his fingers and adept at inserting himself through the smallest of gaps.

Sergeant Roughead brought him up. He said, "Mick wants to see you, Skipper. He thinks we've got some property which belongs to him."

"It's the money you found, if it's the truth I've been told, at the premises of Mr Hinn."

"Quite true," said Petrella. "We did find some money there. Quite a lot of money. You say it was yours?"

"He was minding it for me."

"Was he minding the other things as well?"

"Now what other things would those be?" said Mick, looking at Petrella out of guileless eyes of Irish blue.

"One or two little trifles. Someone seems to have removed them from jewellers' shops without going through the formality of paying for them."

"The world is full of dishonest craytures," said Mick. "I wouldn't know anything about that sort of thing. It's the money I was interested in."

"Have you any sort of proof it belonged to you?"

"Something in writing, you mean. Mr Hinn couldn't write his own name. It's a known fact."

"If there's nothing in writing — " said Petrella. Mick made a very slight movement with his head. Petrella understood it. He said, "That'll be all for now, Sergeant." Sergeant Roughead removed himself unwillingly. He was a student of human nature and Mick was one of his favourite characters.

When the door had closed and Sergeant Roughead's footsteps had died away down the passage, Mick leaned forward, his large hands on Petrella's desk, and said softly, "If you'd care to spend five hundred pounds of that money."

"What would I buy with it?" said Petrella equally softly.

"I'll sell you the Pole."

*

Detective Superintendent Watterson said, "He's got a nerve. Five hundred pounds."

"For the Pole."

"For the Pole," agreed Watterson.

The Pole, sometimes referred to as Augie the Pole, was a man that both Watterson and Petrella would have given a lot of money to put away.

Neither of them had ever set eyes on him. He was a denizen of Little Baltic. He was an unknown quantity. He was a name.

It was a name which a number of people had cause to loathe and to fear.

There had been protection rackets before. Shopkeepers and restaurant proprietors had sometimes paid sums of money under threat that their premises would be disrupted if they refused. More often they had jibbed and asked for police protection. This had led, sooner or later, to a noisy finale and the temporary closing down of the racket. The Pole did not attack premises. He attacked families. Your wife was alone in the house whilst you went out to work. Did you fancy coming home at night and finding her unconscious on the floor with two black eyes and a broken rib? Or maybe you had children. Odd things could happen to children, particularly to young girls. One or two people had complained to the police. Nothing had happened to them, or their families, for several months. The Pole was a patient man. Then he had sent out two of his countrymen. They came, in the early dusk, wearing silk stocking masks and carrying axe-handles or cleavers and they broke up things and people. How many preferred to pay? Petrella had no means of knowing. The Pole never appeared himself. He sent his friends. Their best hope was that some day they would catch one of them red-handed and he might be induced to talk.

"If Mick could put a finger on him," said Petrella, "and give us some solid evidence, it'd be worth paying for."

"Paying for, certainly," said Watterson. "But five hundred pounds!" Petrella knew that the pounds disbursed to informers were counted in tens and twenties. Twenty-five was the most he had ever paid out himself.

"It's not as though it was coming out of police funds," said Petrella.

Watterson said, "That's all very well. Sooner or later someone's going to lay claim to that money. We can't just throw it around as if it belonged to us."

The next claimant arrived that afternoon, in the form of a stout little lady, tightly cased in old-fashioned black. She had read the story of Fred Jury and Johnny Tredgett's discovery. She was, she said, the lawful and only wedded wife of Leopold Hinn. She laid her credentials on the table. They seemed to establish her identity.

She had parted from Leopold some years before, but there had been no divorce. Therefore, he could not lawfully have married again. Therefore, if he was dead, and had left no will, all his goods belonged to her.

Petrella said, "There are two difficulties. The first is that we don't know that he's dead. The second is that we have no means of being certain that the money you are talking about belonged to him."

"Of course it belonged to him," said Mrs Hinn. "It was found behind a looking-glass in his office. It said so in the newspaper."

"Certainly. But he had been there for less than two years. It could have been left there by a previous tenant."

Mrs Hinn said, "You are talking nonsense. No one would leave such money behind them, unless they were dead. I shall speak to a lawyer. He will make you give up the money."

A third claimant announced himself by telephone on the following morning. It was Samuel Lempard. He said, "I've been talking to my solicitor. In fact, he's here with me now. He says that when Hinn gave up — what's that?" Petrella could hear someone prompting him in the background. "Surrendered, yes. When he surrendered the lease he specifically surrendered the contents of the office as well. He's reminded me, that's how we were able to sell the furniture."

"And the document he signed actually says that?"

"In black and white."

"Have you got it there?"

"Right on my desk."

"I'd better come and look at it," said Petrella.

He was on the point of leaving when Sergeant Blencowe appeared. He said, "We've had a get-well card."

It was a dirty piece of paper, in a dirty envelope. The words on the paper had been printed in capital letters, in purple ink. It said, "Mick keeps his stuff in his mother's house in Gosport Lane. It's under the coal in the shed at the end of her garden."

Holding it in his hand, Petrella walked across to one of his filing cabinets and took out a folder. It contained half a dozen letters, all on dirty scraps of paper, all printed in capital letters in purple ink. They were threatening letters which the recipients had brought round to Patton Street.

"It's the Pole all right," said Sergeant Blencowe. "If he's shopping Mick, he must have known Mick was ready to shop him. When thieves fall out, eh?"

"Check up on that coal-shed first. You'll need a warrant. If you find the goods there, pull Mick in." He thought about Mick. "You'd better take a driver and another man with you."

"Mick won't give no trouble. But if the stuff is on his mum's premises, not on his, how are we going to charge him?"

Petrella said, "He won't let his mother stand the racket. He's fond of her."

He was thinking about Mick as his driver inched the car through the thick traffic in Kentledge Road. He was thinking about his two brothers, nearly as big as Mick, and about the small white-haired woman who was the mother of the three. He had a weakness for the Irish. He wished they had taken up Mick's offer when he made it and gone after the Pole. It would have been a lot more satisfactory that way round.

The policeman on point duty recognised the car and held up the traffic for them whilst they turned into Kentledge Mews. They squeezed in behind a large blue station-wagon parked in front of an unmarked door which, Petrella assumed, led up to Mr Lempard's office. The door was locked.

He walked round to the front of the building and took the lift up to the first floor. Here he found Mr Lempard and, lounging in a chair in front of the electric fire, his legal adviser, Eric Duxford.

"Good of you to come round," said Mr Lempard. "Have a drink?"

"Not just now."

"Show him the paper, Duxford."

Eric Duxford uncoiled himself from the chair. He had a long white face, made longer by a pointed beard. He smiled thinly at Petrella. He had been a thorn in the flesh of the South London police for twenty years.

"I think the wording is quite clear," he said. "It's at the top of page two. 'In consideration of the remission of any rental then due and a release from all obligations arising from his tenancy or occupation of the room on the fifth floor of Radnor House in Endless Street the tenant surrenders to the Landlord the said room and all fixtures fittings furniture and other contents thereof.'"

Petrella took the document across to the window and read it through slowly. He was particularly interested in the last page, which was some inches shorter than the other two. Ignoring Mr Duxford's outstretched hand he walked across to Mr Lempard, holding the paper so that the last page only was visible and said, "You say that Mr Hinn signed this in your office one evening."

"So he did."

Petrella could see the tell-tale flush creeping up again.

"And I see that you witnessed his signature."

"That's right."

"Which means that you actually saw him writing his name."

"That's right."

"Then why hasn't he done so?"

There was a moment of absolute silence. Mr Duxford said, "I don't understand you, Inspector — "

Petrella swung round on him and said savagely, "I advise you to keep out of this," and swung back on Mr Lempard.

"I'm going to ask you once again, and I advise you to be very careful about what you say. Did Mr Hinn sign this document in your presence?"

Mr Lempard seemed to be finding some difficulty with his breathing. In the end he said, in a voice so thick that they could scarcely make out the words, "Of course he bloody did. I told you."

Petrella pointed to the straggling letters "L. Hinn", stretching in an almost illiterate scrawl across the paper. He said, "I suppose you thought that was how Mr Hinn would write his name."

"Really, Inspector," said Eric Duxford. "I'm not sure what you're insinuating. It's well known that he was practically illiterate — "

"All that was known about him," said Petrella, "was that he chose to initial documents with a personal hieroglyphic. Quite a common practice in some countries. When he *did* have to write his name, on an official paper for instance, he was perfectly capable of doing so." As he spoke he was laying on the desk in front of the lawyer the documents which Mrs Hinn had produced. These were a form of application to the Home Office for naturalisation dated two years previously, a ten-year-old passport in their joint names and a certificate of marriage. Mr Duxford stared at them, his face nearly as white as his client's.

"You will observe," said Petrella, "that not only does he write his name in a characteristic but perfectly legible hand, but he also spells it in the Nordic way, Hynn."

Both men looked at Mr Lempard, but he seemed to be incapable of speaking.

Petrella said, "I must warn you that a very serious charge may be made against you. A charge of forgery. Mr Duxford will advise you about your rights."

Mr Lempard stared at him without speaking. Petrella could see his lips moving.

"What first gave you the idea that it might be murder?" said Watterson.

"It was a tiny thing," said Petrella. "When I told him he was likely to be charged with forgery, I'll swear his first reaction was relief."

"Try explaining that to a jury."

"And why did he cut off the bottom of the last page? Obviously because there were bloodstains on it."

"Always supposing he did cut it off."

"And look at those two tiny spots, close to the signature. There. One of them looks almost like a full stop. If you hold them up to the light you can see a sort of reddish tinge."

Watterson held the paper up to the light and said, "*If* they're spots of blood the Laboratory will tell us quick enough. But suppose they are. What does it amount to? They could have come from a cut finger or a nose bleed. They don't add up to murder."

"I'm not sure that it was murder," said Petrella. "My guess would be that Mr Hinn agreed to the money that was offered to him — or said he was going to agree. The document was got ready and when he went round to sign it that night he changed his mind. Perhaps he thought he could squeeze a bit more money out of the situation. Lempard's a big man and he's got a hair-trigger temper. I think he hit Mr Hinn a lot harder than he meant, and found himself with an unsigned document and a dead man on his hands."

"Since you've been gazing into the crystal ball," said Watterson sourly, "perhaps you can tell me what he did with the body?"

"If the first part's right, there's not much doubt about the next bit. He'd pick the little man up, carry him down those private stairs and put him into the back of the station-wagon. He'd need a bit of luck there, but it was dark and there wouldn't be many people about in the Mews at that time of night."

"And then?"

"Drop it in the river, dump it in Epping Forest, bury it in his own garden."

Watterson thought about it. He said, "It's full of ifs and buts and guesswork and precious little hard evidence. I can tell you straight away that the Director won't underwrite a murder charge on the strength of one hunch and two drops of blood." He thought about it some more. Petrella waited patiently. He knew his man.

Finally Watterson grunted and said, "All right. *If* the Laboratory says these spots are human blood, we might have enough to justify a few precautionary measures. Lempard's house is in 'P' Division. I could ask Haxtell to have it watched."

"I don't think he'll try to bolt," said Petrella. "He's got too much sense."

Many of his guesses were shortly to be proved right, but over this one he was wrong.

A month later, as proceedings leading to a charge of forgery ground slowly forward, with reports from handwriting experts and statements from Mrs Hinn and others, Lempard decided to leave. He had made a number of discreet preparations and on a rainy night towards the end of April he drove to Heathrow

Airport, unaware that a car was following him and that a telephone message had gone before him. The proceedings at the airport were brisk and, for Mr Lempard, uncomfortable. He could offer no explanation of why he was carrying ten thousand pounds in Swiss notes under the lining of his suitcase and a quantity of small but very valuable diamonds embedded in two cakes of soap in his sponge bag.

A search warrant was now felt to be justified. The body of little Mr Hinn was discovered, four feet down, in the rose-bed at the foot of Mr Lempard's well-kept garden and Mr Lempard was charged with his murder.

Mrs Hinn's claim to the money was conceded. Grudgingly and after considerable pressure, she gave up ten per cent of it to the finders, Fred Jury and Johnny Tredgett, who spent most of it in a celebration party which ended with both of them in the cells of Patton Street Police Station, charged with being drunk and disorderly and assaulting the police.

Petrella took very little part in these final transactions. By that time other matters were occupying his attention fully.

OUT FOR THE COUNTESS:
A Story of Operatic Revenge

Antonia Fraser

"*Dove sono . . .*"questioned the dulcet plangent voice of Emily Nissaki towards the end of the third act of *The Marriage of Figaro*. And: "Where indeed are they, those previous happy moments?" silently echoed Leila Hopper from the third row of the stalls.

"*Dove andaro i giuramenti . . .*" sang the handsome black-haired American soprano, in the role she was rapidly making her own. And: "Too right, where have they gone, those vows of a deceiving tongue?" recited Leila bitterly to herself. She felt at that moment that she had all too much in common with the Countess Almaviva, since both of them faced a predicament caused, essentially, by an unfaithful man.

"Oh heavens! To what humiliation am I reduced by a cruel husband!": those words also had found a tragic echo in Leila Hopper's heart. Except that Leila intended to deal with her own off stage predicament rather differently. No masquerade for her, no changing clothes with her maid — what maid? Leila didn't have a maid — and above all no sweet reconciliation at the end of the day.

"*Più docile io sono . . .*" Yes, the forgiving Countess on stage was going to be a good deal kinder to her husband than Leila was going to be to Charlie Hopper. For what Leila had in mind was murder.

Not the murder of Charlie himself however: reared on the fine old tradition of operatic vengeance, Leila planned something subtler, crueller and finally, she hoped, more devastating. For Leila intended that at the post-opera party in the theatre bar — for the theatre's patrons — Charlie should personally administer poison to his mistress. Not for nothing had Leila thrilled to the macabre and tragic plight of Rigoletto, convinced the wayward Duke was in the sack which actually contained the body of his daughter. And then there were the twists of the plot of *Tosca* by which the singer finally delivered her own lover's death warrant. Charlie Hopper should hand the poisoned chalice — actually the free glass of wine for the patrons — to Magdalen Belport. Thus he would always know that he personally had brought about her agonising death.

What about Leila's own position in all this? Did she really expect to elude discovery for very long? It was true that she had persuaded Charlie in one of his good-husbandly moments to purchase the poison in question on her behalf. (A peculiarly nasty garden potion destined to reduce errant lawns to scorched earth, it was accompanied by a list of warnings which had caused Charlie to observe mildly: "What price the ecology these days, darling?" But when Leila had retorted: "If you weren't away so much and helped me more in the garden . . ." Charlie had dumped the poison and hastily changed the subject.) Since Charlie had indubitably purchased the poison, it would be Charlie's word against hers when it came to the question of who had actually administered it.

At the same time, more grandly, Leila did not expect and did not want to avoid discovery for very long for the crime of passion she was about to commit. After all, what did life hold for her, now that she had lost Charlie?

"*J'ai perdu mon Eurydice* . . ." — Leila adored Gluck — even if she was an unlikely Orpheus and Charlie, handsome broad-shouldered Charlie, an even more improbable Eurydice.

But Magdalen Belport, of all women in the world! It was not that Magdalen Belport lacked beauty: whatever the merits of the late Earl of Belport, who died childless some years ago leaving Magdalen, his fourth much younger wife, a large fortune and the right to queen it at Belport Park for her lifetime, he had known how to pick one who would in a sense grace the role of Countess. Previous Countesses had been renowned for their looks in periods which stretched back into the Thirties. Magdalen, a former model (as the newspapers never failed to point out) had the long fine legs, the narrow hips and neatly catlike features of her original profession. With her elegant unchanging leanness — she had to be well over forty — and an endless fund of money at her disposal, Magdalen Belport could cut more dash at a Patron's function in a pair of white silk trousers and a sequinned matador's jacket than all the other women in more conventional evening dress. Leila knew. She had seen her do it. . . .

No, the fearful cruelty of Charlie's behaviour lay in the relative positions of Leila Hopper and Magdalen Belport within the Festival organisation. And who knew the facts of this better than Charlie himself? As Countess of Belport, by far the most glamorous local figure, Magdalen acted as titular Chairman of the Festival Committee. This meant that she attended at least one Committee meeting, and bought a great many tickets (some of which she always gave away, whether she attended the performance or not, since Magdalen's friends were not exactly passionate lovers of the opera). If Magdalen did attend, she could be guaranteed to behave with the utmost benevolence, glittering matador jacket and all, and make remarks which were on the whole gracefully innocuous — Magdalen liked to please. Then she always went on to accept all the credit for the work of the Festival. That was the work which had actually been carried out, dutifully, devotedly, day in day out, or so it often seemed, by Leila Hopper.

Leila's love of opera might be verging on the obsessional — she knew in her heart of hearts that it was — but then, so she had always thought, was Charlie's own passion for the subject. And yet he had not appreciated the sheer disloyalty of an affair with Magdalen Belport. It was as though to denigrate all their shared feelings for the Festival, the pooled task of finding singers, arranging programmes, in all of which Charlie had so often said: "You *are* the Belport Festival. Don't worry about the public, thank you. Magdalen Countess of B. is just our essential figurehead, a publicity-mad mermaid on the prow of our ship."

Given Charlie's essentially lighthearted temperament, the wayward nature which Leila both loved and deplored, she had often thought that a passion for opera was the deepest, most stable thing in her husband's life. Had it not drawn them together in the first place — that magic evening at the Coliseum listening to Linda Esther Gray as Isolde? Yes, opera was Charlie's greatest passion — until his passion for Magdalen Belport, that is.

"My lovely Countess": Leila would always remember how she found out: those words overheard on the telephone when Charlie had imagined she was working late in her tiny Festival office, following immediately on the highly disquieting incident of the trip to Venice. Charlie Hopper had always travelled a great deal, mainly to America, since his work as a rather grand kind of salesman demanded it, and Leila, since she had no choice, accepted the fact. Charlie did after all in consequence get to hear of rising young stars in the States who might be prepared to visit Belport: that was part of the way in which the Festival work had drawn travelling Charlie and homebound Leila together. (Emily Nissaki, whom Charlie had heard sing Mimi while in Chicago, was an example of that kind of happy serendipity between husband and wife.)

What she did not accept, could never accept, and was now going to take violent action to end, was Charlie's new passion for Magdalen, which meant that since the Venetian trip — as it turned out to be — he had hardly seemed to cast an affectionate glance in Leila's direction, let alone a caress. No Micaela bewailing her lost happiness with Don José had ever felt more piercing sorrow than Leila recalling how long it was since Charlie last made love to her.

"Charlie Hopper! Last seen in Harry's Bar in Venice!" Odd that those seemingly innocent words of international travelling snobbery could have destroyed Leila's peace of mind forever. It was some party at Belport Park in aid — as usual — of fund-raising for the Festival. Leila did not know the man concerned, a big man with receding brown curly hair and a well-cut suit which probably concealed rather too many years of good living. At Harry's Bar, Venice, and elsewhere.

Now Charlie had never, so far as Leila knew, been to Venice; the reason she thought she knew this was that La Fenice was one of those opera houses, described but never visited, which they had both yearned to see for themselves. The person who had been to Venice, many times, no doubt, but certainly very

recently, was Magdalen Belport. In her generous way she had
even brought Leila a present back — some elegant gold and glass
beads (what treachery that now seemed! Leila had since smashed
them up to pieces). The necklace was intended, Magdalen said, as
a thank you to Leila for all the hard work she had done in the run-
up to the present Festival.

"Harry's Bar?" questioned Charlie; he was using his lying
voice; Leila who loved him could tell immediately. "I don't get it."

But Magdalen interrupted him. Unlike Charlie, she spoke
rather too fast, as if concerned to override whatever Charlie might
be going to say.

"Venice!" she exclaimed. "Don't you remember? We bumped
into each other. There was that vast mass of people, all making a
terrible noise, a lot of Italians, well, I suppose that was hardly
surprising. You were alone. I was with a large party."

"Oh, Venice," said Charlie after a pause as though he had
somehow thought the conversation to be about quite another
place, New York, Boston, Chicago (to name three cities he had
recently visited). He gazed steadily at Magdalen, which meant of
course that he avoided looking at Leila. "Harry's Bar in *Venice*,"
he repeated, still staring at Magdalen with that yearning intensity.

Later that night, Leila was first of all informed by Charlie that he
had only briefly visited Venice from Munich (where he also
sometimes went on business en route from the United States) and
had hardly thought it worthwhile mentioning to Leila. Then he
changed his story. The truth was, he finally blurted out, after some
hours of talk in which the subject never quite went away, that
Magdalen Belport had asked him to escort her to an opera gala at
La Fenice. She had been let down, she needed an escort — "you
know what she's like" — Charlie had been in Munich, they had
been in touch over some matter to do with the Festival, he had
flown down. There was nothing else to it. Absolutely nothing.
And now would Leila stop all this and leave him in peace?

Charlie Hopper closed the conversation at this point by going
out of the room abruptly and slamming the door. But Leila saw by
the light on the telephone that he went to make a call. It was a call
that lasted some time. And when Charlie did come to bed, once
again he turned away from his wife.

The next morning all he said was: "I thought you might be jealous. Missing out on La Fenice. You can ask Magdalen if you like. Nothing else to it."

Jealous! It hardly seemed an adequate description of her bewildered feelings. Nor did she intend to raise the subject with Magdalen Belport. It was Magdalen who raised it with her the next morning, paying one of her rare visits to the Festival office. She used exactly the same phrase as Charlie had, Leila noticed.

"An escort, darling. Nothing else to it."

"What was it?" asked Leila suddenly and for her, very sharply, so that Magdalen opened her slanting cat's eyes in astonishment.

"The opera!" Leila almost shouted. "What opera did you go to?"

But at this Magdalen merely smiled in her most feline lazy way. "Oh darling, you don't expect me to remember that. But I do know what I wore: grey satin blazer from St Laurent, very pretty with paler grey crape trousers."

It was quite possible, thought Leila rather wearily, that Magdalen was actually speaking the truth.

Then: "My lovely Countess". It was those words, overheard twelve hours later, which finally convinced Leila that the unbelievable had to be believable: her adored Charlie had transferred all the passion of his nature to Magdalen Belport. And after that, of course, in a terrible brutal way, everything began to fit in. Charlie's increasingly obvious desire to please Magdalen, for example, notably during the meetings of the Festival Committee. His flattery of her taste, even her taste in opera and possible singers for the Festival . . . now that was really going too far. "My lovely Countess," perhaps, but knowledgeable about opera never!

"*Contessa, perdono.*" On stage the opera was almost over and the Count, a short fat man with none of Charlie's handsome looks, was asking his wife to forgive him.

"I am kinder: I will say yes," his wife responded in the rather better-looking incarnation of Emily Nissaki. It had always been one of the moving moments in all Leila's canon of opera. No longer. For Charlie Hopper (and Magdalen Belport) there was to be no forgiveness. In a very short time the post-opera party would begin in the theatre bar. And a very short time after that Magdalen, Countess of Belport, would be dead.

How convenient that Leila, as secretary of the Committee, generally looked after the doling out of the patrons' free drink! It was with special care that Leila handed the fatal glass to Charlie in order that he might — equally fatally — pass it on.

"I've got something special for her. She really wants champagne, of course. But this is at least better than the usual plonk. Take it to her."

Then Leila could not resist adding — what madness overtook her when she had held her tongue for so long? — "Take it to your lovely Countess."

For a moment Charlie, now holding the glass, stood staring at Leila. His expression was one of total amazement, followed almost immediately by guilt.

"She knows." That was what his expression said to her, as clear as words. "She's known all the time."

Leila's own expression, which had been momentarily triumphant, changed to blandness.

"Go on, darling, give it to her." It was her usual polite affectionate tone, the tone of an organiser who needs to make everyone happy. "*Figaro* is not exactly short. She must need it."

"She must indeed," replied Charlie levelly, the amazement and the guilt by now well concealed. He turned away. Leila followed the direction of his tall black dinner-jacketed figure, that formal guise which set off his fair English good looks to perfection. She watched Charlie edging his way through the crowd, polite, skilful, not spilling a drop. There he went, remorselessly towards the corner where Magdalen Belport, svelte as ever in one of her embroidered jackets which surely came direct from Christian Lacroix, held court. Despite the crowd which surrounded her, Magdalen Belport looked up to give Charlie a special intimate smile. Leila watched Charlie, holding her breath. Now, now, let him hold out the glass, let him perhaps kiss her on the cheek — for the last time — but let him at least hold out the glass, let his be the hand, let her drink from it —

But wait — No, for God's sake —

"No!" screamed Leila involuntarily. She stopped. "No Charlie, no," she wanted to cry. "Not her. . . ."—

It was too late. Already the wine was coursing down the throat of Emily Nissaki, that pampered throat soon to be closed and silent forever in death, as she flung back her handsome head with its abundant coils of dark hair, the relic of her Greek ancestry, smiling her thanks with her bold black sloe eyes fixed on Charlie Hopper who had handed her the drink.

Beside her, Magdalen Countess of Belport wondered when Charlie Hopper, or at least that hard-working opera-mad wife of his, would bother to bring her a drink. After all she was the Chairman of the Festival. Hadn't there been something about a special glass of wine? Yet Leila had been behaving so curiously lately, sulking really, she who had always been so grateful for everything. Could she possibly have found out about Charlie . . . Magdalen hoped to God she wasn't planning to leave the Festival office or anything drastic like that. Leila was so clever, so inventive.

So when was that special glass of wine coming? The plonk in the theatre bar was famously disgusting, poisonous one might almost say, even if that face the lead singer was now pulling was surely slightly over the top even for a dramatic soprano.

The death of Emily Nissaki, popularly described as being on stage — the theatre bar was surely near enough to count as that — created a predictable sensation. There were those, it is true, who suggested that her macabre ending cast a false retrospective glamour on her actual talent. But then probably none of those critics had heard her sing in person: those few records so far released did not quite do her justice. These same critics had not, for example, as Charlie Hopper had done, ecstatically followed Emily Nissaki round American opera houses — and to Venice — throughout her brief career; following that first *coup de foudre* meeting with her in Chicago.

Finally Charlie had secured, with some quiet manipulation, that "my lovely Countess", as he was wont to call her — a reference to that glorious night together following her performance in *Figaro* at La Fenice — should come to the Belport Festival. (Even if it had involved flattery beyond the call of duty to Magdalen Belport: still remarkable looking, if you like, and a good sort, but altogether too fond of making men into slaves. If Charlie was going to be a slave, it was to an opera singer like Emily Nissaki, not to an idle rich woman.)

To the rest of the spectators, the way in which Leila Hopper, shortly before confessing her crime, cried out: "The wrong Countess!" and then quoted the general exclamation at the end of *Figaro* of "Heavens! What do I see" made no sense. "The wrong Countess": what could that mean? She had known, surely she had known, of Charlie's affair with Emily Nissaki — otherwise why poison her?

She must have known. It was Magdalen Belport, for example, who reported seeing Emily Nissaki and Charlie Hopper together in Venice.

"Not that I told Leila," Magdalen added quickly. "In fact after Geoffrey's gaffe, I tried like mad to cover up for Charlie by pretending he was alone; whereas of course he was hanging round the neck of that wretched singer, Emily Whatnot. And then I backed him up with Leila to the hilt. Some cock and bull story about going to the opera. As if one didn't have better things to do in Venice! Absolutely to the hilt."

It was only Charlie himself, broken not only by the death of Emily but also by the part he had unwittingly played in it, who knew exactly what his wife had meant by her frantic cry of "the wrong Countess". And her use of those words from *Figaro* — "Heavens! What do I see" — when the "right" Countess finally stepped out of the alcove to reveal herself confirmed it to him. (Not that he could ever tell Magdalen Belport, unaware both of Leila's suspicions and of the peril which had threatened her.)

"Take it to your lovely Countess": how could Charlie have looked in any other direction than towards Emily Nissaki? And so in a sense Leila Hopper, self-confessed murderess Leila, did have her operatic revenge.

DESTROYING ANGEL

Judy Chard

The old man stood, patient and humble, his shabby tweed cap folded neatly under one arm, his roughened peasant hands holding the small basket of mushrooms. The lights from the bar of the clubhouse threw the planes and hollows of the Slav face into shadowed relief.

Colonel White, the club secretary, blustered through the glass door.

"Evening, Jan, the steward said you wanted to see me. . . . Ah, mushrooms." He rubbed his podgy hands, his little pig eyes lighting up in greedy anticipation. The old man bowed his head slightly.

"If I might speak with the Colonel. . . .?" His English was awkward and slow. The other nodded impatiently.

"What is it then?"

Jan hesitated as though he found it difficult to capture the words he wanted.

"My garden — where I grow the vegetables and keep my goose — Stanislaus — the wire is taken down and men — they have brought the big machine and plough it up. . . ."

"Bulldozer," the other interrupted. "That's right, the new fairway to the fourteenth green, all been decided a long time ago, told you all about it."

"I not clearly understand. It is the whole of my vegetable piece, where I grow my plants for market, my wife has a stall there. It is our — how you say? — our living. That, and the mushrooms and fungus which grew in the spinney at the bottom. They have cut down the beautiful silver birch. . . ."

"Yes, well, I'm very sorry about your garden, but as I told you at the time, you people are very lucky to have that camp there to live in. After all, many displaced persons are much worse off than you."

The old man lowered his eyes. His people had been used for generations to being in a constant state of war and upheaval. The nationality of the invaders might change from Mongols to Turks, from Swedes to Prussians, it mattered little.

His own piece of land had been absorbed into a collective farm under the bloodless revolution in 1956. He and his wife had come to England, where their son had already established his own business. And at last they had found peace in the big Polish camp — but now it seemed the roots they had so carefully tended were once more to be torn from the earth.

The Colonel held out his hand. "Thanks for the mushrooms. How much do I owe you?" He fumbled in his pocket.

"I take no payment," the old man said heavily. "The land is now the Colonel's."

White gave a high pitched neigh of a laugh.

"Hardly mine, old man. It's the property of the Tormount Golf Club. Here's half a dollar, anyway, buy yourself a pint of slivovitz or vodka, whatever it is you drink."

Jan ignored the proffered coin with dignity.

"There is one thing I shall tell the Colonel."

"Well?"

The September evening was growing chilly and White had a double scotch waiting on the bar. He stood with ill-concealed impatience.

"On that piece of land, where the beautiful birch trees grew, the mushrooms — they will come again now the machine has gone, and also the fungus, that which is called the Destroying Angel. It is difficult to tell between the two, many people cannot. To eat them is to die."

"Yes, yes, we'll be very careful, if in any doubt, we'll consult you," he said with heavy humour. Really, one had to treat these people like children, or mental defectives. He made a point of not getting involved in other people's problems.

He took the little basket with the gleaming white mushrooms, his mouth watering in anticipation of their succulent juicy flavour with his breakfast bacon.

Jan walked slowly away, oblivious of the beauty of the crimson sun setting behind what was left of the spinney, throwing the slender trees into black relief.

He was thinking with longing of the sleepy village in Little Poland, where he had been born, of his geese and his pig, all that he had left behind among the blossoming fruit trees. And now there would not even be enough grass for the one goose they had — old Stanilaus — his wife's pet.

He hung his cap behind the door, and without troubling to wash his hands, huddled into the old armchair with the broken springs. He pushed away the plate of vegetable stew that Anna, his wife, ladled out and set before him, and sat staring into space.

She shook her head sadly, and picked up the hoe from behind the dresser. The little patch left in front of the door might grow a few onions.

An hour later, when she came to make the coffee, she found him still in the same position, but his head had fallen forward on to his chest, and a little trickle of saliva ran from the corner of his mouth.

The clang of the ambulance bell driving through the Nissen huts of the camp reached the brightly lit bar of the club house like a faint knell from another world. A haze of blue smoke swirled above the heads of the members, who were absorbed in discussion of the new fairway.

The whole affair had been highly controversial. Several committee members had been brought close to resignation. Feeling still ran high.

Some said the old flooded area should have been properly drained, as it was a perfect two hundred and seventy yarder, and suited their play. Others, that the new fairway, which approached the green up a slight incline, was a two shotter for the medium and low handicappers, and the making of the almost perfect course.

Those who were against had used Jan and his garden as an extra lever in their argument.

But to White the mere existence of the Polish camp was a festering sore. It ran alongside most of the thirteenth fairway, tatty with rusting wire and corrugated iron, the rough scrub and brambles the other side of the fence a haven for rabbits, which came on to the fairway and nibbled bare patches, and the seepage from the drains, which caused the flooding of the fourteenth.

From long years of habit, the Colonel was an early riser. He loved the course in the morning, when no one else was about, and he hadn't missed the significance of Jan's remarks that the mushrooms were coming again where the spinney had been. He was determined no one else should get them.

As he walked through the clear, dewy morning, his eyes rested with pride on what he considered the finest stretch of golfing country in England, perfect undulating turf, winding wooded pathways, and velvet greens where the little red flags gleamed and fluttered in the breeze.

When he reached the new fairway he was annoyed to see someone was before him. A short, squat figure, walking heavily and stooping frequently as though picking something from the ground.

As he drew near he saw an old woman with a black shawl round her head, a basket on her arm, wandering among the stumps of the spinney at the end of the new fairway. She straightened up and stood still, watching him approach.

Behind her was the new wire fence, close against the wall of one of the nissen huts. He noticed the bright paint and cheap, flowered curtains at the small windows.

"Sir," she said. It was neither question nor greeting. A statement of fact, and said so softly he was not sure if she had spoken at all.

"You must go back to the camp," he said sharply. Something about her attitude was disquieting. "People will be playing here very soon. You may get hit."

"It is Jan, my husband. We live here. . . ." She vaguely indicated the Nissen hut.

"What about Jan?" he asked.

"He was taken ill. The ambulance come."

"Oh, I'm sorry to hear that. What's the trouble?"

"It is his heart."

"Don't worry too much, they can do wonderful things these

days. Just as well you've got less ground to dig now," he said smugly. "Anyway you're lucky to be in England where the hospital is free."

"No hospital can cure what he has," she said softly, as though to herself.

"Nonsense," he said sharply. "You can't possibly know that."

"I know. I am a woman. His wife. I know about these things. His heart is broken."

"Rubbish! No such thing. I'm very sorry to hear about his trouble, but I'm sure rest and treatment will see him better very shortly."

She held out the basket. "Jan tell me you fond of the mushroom."

He was slightly taken aback. "Oh — thanks — thanks very much." He took a coin from his pocket. "Give my regards to Jan, and buy him some grapes."

As he took the basket from her he was shocked for the moment to see the undisguised malice in the black eyes.

He forgot the incident as he returned to the club house and found the local doctor waiting for a round of golf.

He hadn't much time for him. Drank too many dry martinis, and out on the course when he should have been attending to his practice. No dedication to duty in his opinion. Only the other day he'd said to him, "A round a day keeps the doctor away—from his patients." He'd thought it funny, but the doctor hadn't laughed.

It was after midnight when he eventually reached home. As he got out of the car he caught sight of the basket of mushrooms on the back seat. He decided to fry a few for his supper. He was a bachelor. "A wife is an expensive luxury," he'd always said, and he was quite capable of looking after himself. That way he could have his meals when he wanted. After he had eaten he suddenly felt very tired and went to bed, leaving the dishes in the sink.

Just before dawn he woke with violent pains in his stomach. He struggled to the kitchen to make himself a cup of tea. As he stood at the sink filling the kettle, his legs gave way under him. He grabbed the draining board and his fingers caught in the handle of the basket which had held the mushrooms. Two small ones were left in the bottom, and they rolled on to the floor.

Suddenly cold panic seized him. The mushrooms that old crone had given him!

Suppose they'd been those other things, the toadstools. What had Jan called them?

Destroying Angels. Maybe the old woman hadn't her husband's knowledge and had picked some by mistake.

A worse thought occurred to him — perhaps she had known. It was revenge for Jan's illness. Damned foreigners were all the same, hysterical and unreliable. He always said sympathy with them didn't pay. He must be getting soft, feeling sorry for the old fool.

The pain in his chest and stomach eased a little. He struggled to a chair. Perhaps it was just indigestion from eating so late.

He'd never had a day's illness in his life. No time for people who fussed over their health. Good day's work soon put them right. It was all in the mind.

His breathing had been a bit difficult lately though. Maybe he ought to have a check up. He hadn't even got a regular doctor. Only one he knew was that lazy oaf at the club.

While the kettle boiled he'd have a look in that encyclopædia in the other room, see if those things really did exist. Probably a figment of the old fool's imagination.

He got the book down from the shelf and ran his finger along the index. Fungi — yes, there they were with a drawing. "Destroying Angel, or Death Cap. Mushroom-like in size and appearance, but the gills are creamy, not brown, and there is a volva at the base of the stem."

He read on: "There are no symptoms of poisoning for from six to twenty hours after, which precludes any normal method of expulsion from the stomach being used. There is violent stomach ache. . . ."

As though in sympathy with the printed words, another spasm of pain seized him, more excruciating than the first. There was a bitter taste in his mouth. Fear — stark and cold, followed by blinding anger at having trusted another human being, filled him as he staggered to the phone.

Frantically he searched the directory for the doctor's number. It was a full minute before a woman's voice answered. The words tumbling over each other, he explained what had happened, what he suspected.

"My husband is out on a maternity case, I can't really say how long he'll be, but I'll ring the hospital for an ambulance," she said.

"Tell them to hurry." His voice was thick with terror and fury at everyone's incompetence.

The pain subsided a little as he rang off. He sipped some of the tea, his hands trembling so much that he spilt the boiling liquid on his leg.

He'd have that woman up for attempted murder. His palms were sweating, but his body felt ice cold. He had difficulty in moving his left hand . . . why didn't somebody come. . . .

Suddenly the pain gripped him again like a vice. It had moved to the left side of his chest. His heart beats were loud and the pounding of his blood through his pulses like the throbbing of an engine.

A great darkness slapped into his eyes. . . .

The Colonel's death caused quite a stir at the club, but he had never been popular, and the whole matter was soon eclipsed by the fact that the new fairway got flooded just the same as the old one had — worse if anything.

It was decided to move the wire back again and drain the land properly, which, but for the Colonel, would probably have been done in the first place.

When Anna took the news to Jan in hospital it brought the colour back to his pale face. The rest too had done him good. In a few days he was back home again.

It didn't take long to re-cultivate the land torn up by the bulldozer. But, of course, only time could replace the birch wood.

Stanislaus, the goose, had been reprieved from the pot and stood, as truculent as ever, on his patch of newly seeded grass.

The inquest on the Colonel was only a formality, for the post mortem showed he'd died of a stroke.

A DANGEROUS THING, MRS CRAGGS

H.R.F. Keating

A certain number of the cleaning jobs that Mrs Craggs had at one time or another in the sprawling conglomeration of London took her into places which it is not given to everyone to enter. Perhaps the one of these that she liked the best was the Reading Room at the British Museum.

Of course, she saw little of the Reading Room while it was properly in use, when the Readers were there deep in volumes from that huge collection to which by law every single book, magazine, fascicle or pamphlet published in Great Britain must be sent. But she liked the stately, quiet atmosphere of the huge round chamber under its shallow glass dome as she polished its great floor early in the mornings before the hour of opening. She liked the encircling shelves of leather-smelling tomes, the *British Union Catalogue of Periodicals*, the *Bibliothèque Nationale Catalogue des Imprimés*, the *Cumulative Book Index*, the *Annual Register*, the *Calendars of State Papers*, Halsbury's *Statutes of England*, *Notes and Queries* and the long run of *The Gentleman's Magazine*. And she very much liked what she saw of the learned people who began to come in at 9.30 a.m.

They might not, she would often think, be any great shakes as specimens of physical beauty, running as they did for the most part to shoulders stooped and rounded by long hours bent over volumes laid out on desks and to posteriors more adapted to the seated attitude than to the soldierly march or the elegance of the dance. But, by and large, the love of their work, the love of scholarship for the sake of scholarship, shone in their eyes, gleamed clearly through spectacle lenses often neglectfully smeared. And Mrs Craggs, though she was the first to acknowledge that she was not usually much of a reader herself, loved them for that.

Not that she loved every single one she chanced to see after her chief duty of polishing that enormous circular floor with its radiating spokes of Readers' desks was over and she was occupied in seeing to parts of the huge learning machine not open to the public, even to that privileged section of them in possession of Readers' Admission Tickets. There were a few individuals she had picked out as being, for all their industry at their desks, not proper scholars, not people dedicated to the pursuit of knowledge for its own sake. Most of these "whizzers", as Mrs Craggs called them in her own mind, were comparatively young, though they were not all necessarily so. And she would have had difficulty, had she been asked, in saying just what it was about them that marked them out for her.

Perhaps it was the way they always hurried. They hurried to be first in the short queues waiting to hand in book application slips at the small circular area that forms the hub of the Room's great wheel. They hurried, first thing in the morning, to occupy some particular one of the 390 blue-leather-covered desks which they considered to be nearest the particular reference works on the Room's perimeter that they might need. They hurried, when closing time came, to be first in the queues to hand back their books for safe keeping during the night. "Whizzers", in Mrs Cragg's eyes, spoilt the slow, quiet, studious atmosphere of the place much as a garish half-squashed Coke can spoils the beauty of some ancient close-mown lawn on to which it has been carelessly thrown.

Once she overheard one of her gentlemen, one of the ones who was certainly not a whizzer, quoting a couple of lines of poetry to himself as he toddled away to get some lunch at midday.

> "A little learning is a dang'rous thing;
> Drink deep, or taste not the Pierian spring."

She had often wondered what the heck a Pierian spring was, but she had had no difficulty in at once agreeing with the bit about "a little learning". It was a dangerous thing, she knew that in her bones. And it was the whizzers who had it, and would be dangerous some day to someone somewhere.

Before long there came a time when she had startling proof of this. It was on a day that began no differently from any other. Except for one funny thing.

Mrs Craggs had been standing at the entrance to the Reading Room in the lofty inner hall of the vast Museum itself, talking to a friend of hers, one of the warders who check people going in to make sure they are in possession of a Reader's Ticket. It was a slack time, shortly after the first small rush of Readers when the Museum opens, and Mr Meiklejohn, a Scot who had lost none of his Scottishness for long residence in London, had been glad of a few moments' chat. They had just got on to the subject of whizzers, though Mrs Craggs was keeping her pet name for them to herself, and Mr Meiklejohn, who was a pretty formidable scholar himself — if the faces of Readers, past, present, long-term and temporary, is a subject for scholarship — was agreeing that there were "bodies you can pick out who are never your regular Reader the way a Reader ought tae be", when a very, very elderly man came slowly, slowly up to the entrance.

He looked, thought Mrs Craggs, about as old as anybody could be. He had a little stooped frail body that shuffled forward under an enormous old overcoat, despite the summer heat, like a tortoise in its shell. His head, on which a few white hairs were spread this way and that, poked out on the end of a scrawny, thin length of neck round which an old grey woollen muffler was wrapped. And he surveyed the world cautiously through a pair of tiny glinting pince-nez spectacles.

Mr Meiklejohn stepped forward and asked with grave Scottish courtesy if he could see his Reader's Ticket.

"Reader's Ticket?" said the old gentleman, as if such an object were something he had once heard of, dimly. "Reader's Ticket? Well, yes, I suppose I have a Reader's Ticket. Must have been given one when I first used the Library, in '99, I think that must have been. Ninety-nine or '98, can't quite remember."

Mr Meiklejohn shot Mrs Craggs a quick glance of amazement. Could the old boy really be meaning that he had first come to the Reading Room in the year 1899, or even 1898, eighty years ago? Was it possible?

And Mrs Craggs, looking at that peering scaly tortoise head on its long thin desiccated scarf-wound neck, thought that, well, it might be. It might really be. It would make the old boy probably a hundred years old, a bit less if he had begun to come to the Reading Room as a bright lad of eighteen or nineteen, but anyhow within a few months of his century. And he looked old enough to be a centenarian, every bit.

"Have you got your Ticket on you now, sir?" Mr Meiklejohn asked, pitching his voice a wee bit loudly in case the old gentleman was hard of hearing.

"On me? Now? I might have. I suppose I might have. Somewhere. But why on earth do you want to know?"

Mr Meiklejohn strove not to allow too astonished a look to appear on his features.

"We have to examine Reader's Tickets now, sir," he said. "It's a Regulation. Has been for — for a good many years, sir."

"Oh. Oh, I see. Unauthorised fellers trying to make their way inside, eh?"

"Something like that, sir. And there have been thefts, sir, I'm sorry to say."

"Thefts? Thefts, eh? What is the world coming to when a scholar and gentleman will steal from his own Library?"

"Aye, it's a terrible thing, sir. A terrible thing. But I'm afraid it means I'll have to see your Ticket, sir."

"Oh, of course. Of course."

The old gentleman brought one rather trembly grey-woollen-gloved hand to join the other and with extreme slowness plucked off the right-hand glove. He then seemed in some doubt about what to do with it.

"Might I hold that for you, sir?" asked Mr Meiklejohn.

"Oh. Oh, yes. Yes. Good of you."

Mr Meiklejohn secured the grey glove — the tips of its fingers had been carefully darned once, many years ago — and the old gentleman plunged his free hand into the recesses of his overcoat.

A sudden rattling noise, like a quick burst of fire from a Uzi sub-machine gun, came from just behind them. Mrs Craggs and Mr Meiklejohn looked round. It was a Reader, a Reader wanting to enter and coughing to draw attention to his need. And, in that one quick, half-second glance, Mrs Craggs put him down at once as a whizzer, a whizzer plainly in a fury because he was being held up from plunging into the Reading Room and his waiting books.

"One moment, if you please, Mr Tipton-Martin," said Mr Meiklejohn, authority on Readers' faces.

Mr Tipton-Martin, who was about twenty-four or twenty-five, with a pale, slightly fat face and pale, well-brushed hair, wearing not the neglected clothes that most Readers seemed to possess but a well-pressed light blue safari suit with a shirt in broad blue and white stripes to match, gave Mr Meiklejohn a glance of suppressed rage. But there was nothing he could do about getting through the narrow entrance to the Reading Room before the old gentleman.

For perhaps as much as a minute or more the latter fished waveringly inside his overcoat. But then his hand emerged gripping a time-polished leather wallet. With trembling fingers, rather hampered by the grey glove still on his other hand, he attempted to pull out from it a small card that once might have been white but was now grey with age.

"Should I give you a hand, sir?" asked Mr Meiklejohn.

Behind the old gentleman young Mr Tipton-Martin produced a snort of quick disgust.

"That's very good of you," said the old gentleman, handing over the wallet.

Mr Meiklejohn deftly extracted the card and gave it a glance.

"Mr Walter Grappelin," he read. "Thank you, sir."

He was about to slip the card back into the old gentleman's wallet when he suddenly stopped and gave it another scrutiny.

"I'm verra sorry, sir," he said, "but this Ticket's out of date. It doesna' appear to have been renewed since. . . ."

He stopped, and then continued in a voice from which he strove to eliminate the incredulity.

" . . . since 1943, sir."

"Yes," said old Mr Grappelin. "Yes, that would be right. I suppose it must have been a year or so after that I last had occasion to use the Library. Just about the time of the end of the Second World War, the one with that chap Hitler, you know. I retired from my Editorship about then, and the Bodleian at Oxford has been sufficient for my needs up till now. But I found yesterday that I really ought to look up that novel of George Sand that was suppressed, you know, and the Bodleian hasn't a copy. So I thought I'd better come up here."

"Quite so, sir," said Mr Meiklejohn reassuringly. "But I'm afraid you really will have to get your Ticket renewed. The office is just by the main entrance doors down there, sir. Round to your right."

"Ah. Good. Thank you. Thank you."

And the old man shuffled away, moving not much faster than the tortoise he so much resembled.

"Your Ticket, Mr Tipton-Martin, then," Mr Meiklejohn said briskly.

"Oh. Er-er-Ticket? Oh, yes, my Ticket."

Young safari-suited Mr Tipton-Martin seemed not at all his usual whizzing self. Mrs Craggs wondered why.

And, for once, her curiosity was satisfied. Instead of shooting into the Reading Room and zipping round to secure himself some particularly advantageous desk, Mr Tipton-Martin stayed where he was and actually began to gossip with Mr Meiklejohn. To gossip. There was, thought Mrs Craggs, no other word for it.

"Do you know who that was?" he asked the warder.

"Gentleman name of Grappelin, sir."

"Yes. But he's no ordinary gentleman. He's Professor Walter Grappelin. You know, the Editor of the *Oxford Dictionary of Nineteenth-Century French*, one of the great works of scholarship of our time. I thought he was dead years ago. The Dictionary came out in 1945, and he was quite old then. He retired as soon as he'd seen it through the press. He must be damned near a hundred now."

"A verra remarkable man, sir," said Mr Meiklejohn, in suitably awed tones. "Verra remarkable indeed."

Mr Tipton-Martin laughed. It was an unexpected sound. Mrs

Craggs reckoned that whizzers didn't often laugh. But then this seemed to be a day of unexpected events.

"You may say old Walter Grappelin's remarkable," Mr Tipton-Martin said. "But he wasn't half as remarkable as his young brother."

"Indeed not, sir? Then the younger Mr Grappelin must have been verra, verra remarkable."

"He was. He was. He was the poet, you know."

Mr Meiklejohn shook his head.

"I'm not verra much o' what you'd call a poetry man mesel', sir," he said.

"No? I should have thought that everyone had heard of Maurice Grappelin. After all, next to Rupert Brooke he was probably our finest poet of the '14-'18 War."

"Indeed, sir? Weel now, that's verra interesting."

"That's as may be," said Mr Tipton-Martin a little sharply. "But the poetry's by no means the most interesting thing about Maurice Grappelin. Not many people remember this, or even know it. But he wasn't only a poet. He was a remarkable scholar as well. A philologist, of course, in the family tradition, following his elder brother's footsteps. But if you ask me, he'd have far outshone him if he'd lived. If his discoveries in the field of — but, never mind, you'd hardly understand."

"The poor gentleman died early then, sir?" Mr Meiklejohn asked with undeterred sympathy.

"Died early?" Mr Tipton-Martin snapped. "Why, he was killed, man. Killed in 1914. Didn't you even know that?"

"I'm afraid not, sir," Mr Meiklejohn said.

He sounded thoroughly ashamed of his ignorance, and Mrs Craggs, who in the ordinary way would not have ventured to address a Reader, quite suddenly jumped into the conversation.

"An' 'ow come you know such a lot about his philol-whatsit an' all that?" she asked, politeness abandoned.

Mr Tipton-Martin looked affronted. As perhaps he had reason to be, suddenly spoken to by a person in a flowered apron with a rather squashed-looking red hat on her head.

"As a matter of fact," he said, chilliness in every word, "I work in the same discipline myself and I was also privileged, as an undergraduate, to re-catalogue the library at Castle Mandeville, a task which had been abandoned by none other than the young Maurice Grappelin at the outbreak of the 1914-18 War. So naturally I know something of the man, perhaps rather more than any other scholar in the field."

And with that he turned on his heel and flounced into the Reading Room, omitting to show Mr Meiklejohn his Reader's Ticket.

But Mr Meiklejohn was unperturbed. He shook his head wonderingly.

"Losh," he said. "It's always amazing to me just how much a real scholar knows."

Mrs Craggs sniffed.

"Real scholar," she said.

"Och, come now, Mrs Craggs. The wee man's been spoken of as one of the rising people. There was a gentleman the other day who told me that when next month a certain learned journal comes out it's to have an article in it by the young man that's likely to astonish everybody in the field and make his name for him once and for all. Not that anyone else will ken what it's all about, mind. But in his wee world he's fair bent to be a king-pin."

"That's as may be," Mrs Craggs said, not at all impressed by this example of a whizzer whizzing. "But all the same, he only knew all about that Maurice Grappelin 'cos he happened to have had a job in the selfsame place where the feller worked afore he went off an' got shot for his country. I don't see what's so ruddy amazing about that."

The next thing that happened on this day which was to turn out to be extraordinary in every way was that Mrs Milhorne lost her handbag. Mrs Milhorne had been a cleaner in the Reading Room for much the same time as Mrs Craggs had been. But her view of the Readers was not at all the same as her friend's. She regarded them all, scholars and whizzers alike, as creatures of an extraordinary, superior order, as not so much human beings with human beings' imperfections and weaknesses as walking Brains, beyond and above ordinary ways as the stars are above the humdrum earth.

So naturally when she realised she had left her handbag tucked into one of the knee-hole shelves at desk Number F8 when she had dusted it that morning she felt entirely incapable of simply going quietly into the Reading Room and retrieving it.

"I'd disturb them," she said to Mrs Craggs, much as she might have been saying "I'd assassinate them." "I couldn't do it. I couldn't. Me nerves would go all to pieces. I just could not set foot in That Room."

"Then you'll have to manage without your old bag."

"But I must have it. I must. It's got me pills in it. I need them pills. One every four hours I got to take. The Doctor said so."

"Then go in and fetch it."

"I couldn't. I can't. But I must have it. I must."

Mrs Craggs sighed. She had known from the start what would happen in the end.

"All right," she said. "I'll go."

And into the Reading Room with its ranks of bowed studious heads she went, walking quietly as she could but unable, of course, to do anything about her left shoe, which squeaked abominably and always had.

But only one intent reader took any notice, and that was a whizzer, one of the female variety, a lady dressed in a severe grey suit, with a pointed nose and heavy purple-rimmed spectacles. She hissed at Mrs Craggs like an affronted goose. But otherwise nothing stopped her making her way between the radiating spokes of face-to-face desks with their high separating partitions until she got to Number F8.

She recognised its occupant at once. It was the old, old man, Professor Grappelin. He must have succeeded in renewing his Reader's Ticket without any trouble, she thought, and here he was now sitting patiently at this desk waiting for that book he wanted to come from where it must lie in the deep underground bookstores among the rows on rows of close-packed volumes.

Or rather, Mrs Craggs thought, he ain't so much waiting as having a nice bit of a zizz till his book comes. He had, she saw, been reading a magazine, one of them magazines that the learned gents of the Reading Room were always reading. She could see its title. *The Journal of Philological Studies*. Whatever "philological" meant. And she could see the date on it, too. Today's date. The old boy still keeping up with all the latest, even if he was damn nearly a hundred years old.

She decided that she could probably rescue Mrs Milhorne's handbag from the knee-hole shelf without disturbing the old boy. And she would have succeeded in doing so, too. Only, just as she stooped to reach in beside the old chap's unmoving little frail body, a crumpled piece of paper that someone had dropped on the floor just under the desk caught her eye. Tidying-up was a discipline to Mrs Craggs. If there was dirt or mess about she could no more stop herself dealing with it than she could have stopped herself breathing. So she reached down and picked up the piece of paper — it was a sheet of plain paper, very stiff and just lightly squeezed together — and thrust it into the pocket in the front of her flowered apron with the intention of popping it into a wastepaper basket as soon as she had got out of the quietly calm atmosphere of the Reading Room.

But, in reaching just a little further so as to get hold of that piece of rubbish, the edge of her shoulder lightly brushed against the sleeping professor's jutting-out elbow. And when it did so the old, old man, his body weighing hardly more than that of any lucky little girl's giant doll, toppled over out of his chair to lie, just in the position he had been in, curled up on the floor.

Mrs Craggs gasped. And then she gave a little short sharp involuntary scream.

Because, as the old man had fallen, his long grey muffler had come away and, looking down, Mrs Craggs's eyes had been drawn as if by two tugging black threads to the handle of a small shining silver paperknife that was protruding from the back of that frail old tortoise neck.

Mrs Craggs had recovered herself in a moment and had gone straight along to the central round desk to report the murder, all the more disturbed because of a nagging feeling at the back of her mind that somewhere before she had seen the murder weapon, that little silver paperknife. Its handle was funny. In the shape of a stubby, short-armed cross. She had seen that before some-where, couldn't mistake it.

Just as she was about to report she noticed, a yard or two further round the counter, young Mr Tipton-Martin, standing waiting to hand back books he had finished with. So, remembering that he had known who old Professor Grappelin was, she went round, took him by the elbow and marched him back round, despite his initial protests, to help her tell her story.

It was a good thing she had done so, because, once a police constable had been summoned from the courtyard outside the Museum, Mr Tipton-Martin was able to advance matters in a decidedly swift way. Or so it seemed.

"Constable," he said, when things had begun to be sorted out a little and they were waiting for the full might of Scotland Yard to arrive, "there's something I think you ought to know."

"I hesitate to tell you, because it may seem like launching an accusation against a person who may be perfectly innocent. But on the other hand he is still here, and — "

"Who is this, sir?" the constable asked, with some urgency.

Mr Tipton-Martin pulled at the corners of the collar of his smart blue-and-white striped shirt.

"It's Francis Lecroix," he said. "I don't suppose you'll have ever heard of him, officer, but he's quite well known in his field, in a way. He's a philologist. Or he was. Well, he almost certainly still thinks of himself as one."

"I'm sorry, sir," said the constable. "But I don't quite see what you're getting at."

"No? No, I'm sorry. Well, you see, it's quite simple really. Lecroix years ago was one of Professor Grappelin's assistants on his great work, the *Oxford Dictionary of Nineteenth-Century French*. But he quarrelled with him. It was a professional disagreement over the definition of a certain group of words. And he resigned. And then, I'm afraid, he never got another job in the academic world. People thought he wasn't sound, you know. But he still persisted with his notion that Professor Grappelin had committed a serious crime in compiling that section of the Dictionary. He became obsessed with the idea. He even wrote a little book to explain his theories, and had it privately printed and copies sent to every philologist of note. It's very well known in its way, a sort of joke. Because, you see, the

chap is mad, of course. Mad as a hatter. But he happens to be
here in the Reading Room now, and it was today that Professor
Grappelin suddenly surfaced when everybody thought he must
be dead long ago."

"I see, sir," said the constable. "And just where is this other
gentleman now, this Mr — er — Lecroix, was it?"

"He's here, officer. Just there."

And Mr Tipton-Martin extended a long arm and pointed right
over to a far corner, just near Desk P9.

Mrs Craggs, who like everybody else had followed that long
pointing arm, felt a sudden thump of dismay somewhere in the
region of her heart. Because she recognised the man Mr Tipton-
Martin had named. He was the old scholar she had once heard
muttering to himself that "a little learning is a dang'rous thing".
And, worse, the moment she saw him she knew where it was that
she had seen that silver paperknife with the stubby cross handle.
She had seen it more than once. On whatever desk it had been
that Francis Lecroix was occupying. He always had it with him.
He was always reading those old books that had uncut pages and
he used the knife constantly to open them up.

Of course the constable had gone straight over and asked old
Francis Lecroix — he must be seventy-five if he's a day, Mrs
Craggs thought — to step over this way if he would. And there he
had been by the Central Desk when, from Scotland Yard, to take
charge of the inquiry, there had arrived, with an impressive escort
of detective-sergeants and fingerprint men and photographers
and a scene-of-crime officer, the great towering form of Superintendent Mouse.

Mrs Craggs recognised him from his photo in the papers, that
slab-sided six-foot-six-inches body, that solid wall of a face. But
what she had never seen in the papers was what Superintendent
Mouse pulled from the top pocket of his tent-like grey suit when
Mr Tipton-Martin repeated his account of old Professor Grappelin, the *Oxford Dictionary of Nineteenth-Century French* and
Mr Lecroix — a pair of heavy horn-rim spectacles. He put them
on the bridge of his massive squabby nose and peered through
them at little, safari-suited Mr Tipton-Martin.

"Hm," he said. "The *ODNCF*, eh? Masterly piece of work, of

course. I do a little reading on those lines myself from time to time, and I couldn't do without it."

Mr Tipton-Martin positively preened himself.

"Then perhaps you'll know that little book, *The Great Oxford Dictionary of Nineteenth-Century French Scandal*, Lecroix's polemic?" he said.

"Hm. Ha. Yes. Yes, interesting piece of work. In its way."

"But the work of — " Mr Tipton-Martin dropped his voice since old Francis Lecroix was, after all, standing there blinking from one to the other — "a total lunatic."

"Oh, yes, yes. Undoubtedly. Lunatic, yes, lunatic."

Superintendent Mouse removed his heavy hornrims and tucked them decisively into his top pocket.

"Well, thank you, Mr — er — Tupton-Marlowe," he said. "And now I think, Mr Lecroix, if you'll accompany me to Scotland Yard we can have this business cleared up before very much longer."

"Oh, no, you don't," said Mrs Craggs.

She was surprised, really, to hear her own voice, right out loud like that in the tremendous hush that had fallen on the wide-domed Reading Room after the first excitement had died down. But she had spoken. The words had been forced out of her from somewhere.

And she was glad that they had.

But everyone was looking at her now. Superintendent Mouse's ham-like left hand was groping again for his hornrims. She had to justify what she had said.

"Look," she began, "you can't take him away like that. Well, there ain't no need to."

Superintendent Mouse dropped the hornrims, which he had got half-way out of his top pocket, back in. Plainly this was not a matter where the more intellectual side of life could be called into play.

"You're the lady that found the body," he pronounced. "Cleaning woman, isn't it? Mrs Bloggs, I believe."

"If you believe that, you'll believe anything that likes to come into your head," Mrs Craggs retorted. "No, name's Craggs, an' always has been ever since we was united more years ago than I cares to remember. An' if you believe a gentleman like old Mr Lecroix here, what's what I calls a real scholar, could've done what was done to that poor old professor, then you're worse nor what I thought."

Superintendent Mouse drew himself up to his full six-foot-six. The breadth of his body was enormous.

"That's quite enough of that," he said. "When I want a charwoman to tell me who's a scholar and who isn't I'll sell every book in my library. I dare say Mr Lecroix here looks like a scholar to you, clothes he hasn't changed for the best part of six months and spectacles with their left lens cracked, but that doesn't make him any different from any other person or persons. And he's got a little bit of explaining to do back at the Yard."

He turned his massive bulk to face the aged author of *The Great Oxford Dictionary of Nineteenth-Century French Scandal*, who did indeed look a dusty and neglected figure.

"No, just you come along with me," he said.

But Mrs Craggs thrust herself, flowered apron, squashed red hat, between the Superintendent and his prey.

"He ain't going," she said. How she brought herself to say it she never knew. "He ain't going, or not until you've listened to reason for half a minute."

"My good woman."

"Don't you 'good woman' me. An' just you listen. Mr Lecroix is a scholar. Ain't I seen him in here day after day? Nose down in those old books of his? Cutting away at every single page as has been stuck together ever since the book was printed and nobody else cared what was inside?"

But Superintendent Mouse's massive face had suddenly lit up with an inner fire.

"Cutting away at uncut pages?" he said. "And what was he using to do that with? Come along now, speak up."

It was then that Mrs Craggs thought that all she had done was to make matters worse for her nice old gentleman. But it was his knife that was still sticking deep into the frail neck of old Professor Grappelin, and she knew it was. And not telling the truth was not going to make matters one bit better for anyone.

So she told the truth. And Superintendent Mouse put on his heavy hornrims and went over and gave the shiny silver handle of the paperknife a short personal examination.

Then he returned to the Central Desk where the group of them were still standing.

"Yes," he said. "Well, come along now, Mr Lecroix."

Mrs Craggs felt terrible. She knew that old Mr Lecroix, the man who could toddle out of the Reading Room muttering "a little learning is a dang'rous thing", for all that he might have a bit of a bee in his bonnet about some complicated bit of studying in that huge big dictionary they were all on about, could not have plunged his paperknife into the old professor's neck and then covered up its jutting silver handle with the grey muffler. He could not have done that. It wasn't right for a man like him.

But how had his knife, his very own knife in the form of a cross, that she herself had seen him with so often, how could that knife have got to have been used for the horrible purpose that it had, if he was not the person who had used it?

And then she knew.

It came to her in a flash. No, old Mr Lecroix, the real scholar, had not used that knife. It had been used by none other than Mr Tipton-Martin, whizzer. She realised that not only did she know this, but she knew why Mr Tipton-Martin had done what he had done.

No wonder he had gabbled and gabbled on like that after the sudden appearance of the old, old professor when everyone had thought he was long ago dead. Professor Walter Grappelin, whose brother had been Maurice Grappelin, the poet who had been tragically killed in 1914. The poet and the philol-whatsit. A philol-whatsit like Mr Tipton-Martin himself, Mr Tipton-Martin who had once worked in a library somewhere where Maurice Grappelin had been working until he had dropped everything to go and fight in the war. Had left behind — she knew this to be true, as if she had seen the evidence with her own eyes — some discovery or other in philol-whatsit that young Tipton-Martin years later had found. Had found and had pinched, safe in the knowledge that no one would know that Maurice Grappelin had done the work before him. Only, what was more likely than that

Walter Grappelin would recognise his brilliant young brother's work when, just next month, it came out in the *Journal of Philolthingamebob Studies*? The very magazine the old, old man had been reading this month's copy of just before he had fallen asleep at his desk over there.

And young whizzer Tipton-Martin had realised his danger, and then had realised that the perfect scapegoat for the murder that would get him out of his trouble and let him whizz on up to being king-pin of philol-whatsit was there in the Reading Room, asking to be made use of. Even down to providing him with a weapon that would point back to its owner like a ruddy illuminated street-sign.

But how was she to prove all this? How was she to convince Superintendent Mouse when plainly he had lapped up every word that his fellow so-called scholar, young Safari Suit, had ladled out to him?

Old Mr Lecroix had said hardly a word up till now. He had agreed that he was who he was, but beyond that he had kept silent, looking from face to face as each development occurred. But now he spoke.

"Grappelin was wilfully mistaken over the vocabulary of the *midinettes*," he said. "Wilfully, you know. You've only to read my book to see why. But I wouldn't have wished him any harm."

"There," said Mrs Craggs. "There. You see. Mild as Dutch cheese. 'Ow can you say he'd of done a thing like that?"

"Mrs Bloggs," said Superintendent Mouse, "I should be reluctant to have you charged with obstruction, but, believe me, I shall if you persist in this."

His huge left hand reached up to his hornrims as if he would like just to peruse the relevant section of the Act before instituting proceedings.

It's now or never, thought Mrs Craggs. Whatever shall I do?

And then — then, as if the spirit of Athene, goddess of wisdom, had descended on her from the great domed roof above, the answer came to her. She had had it. She had had it all along.

So now she produced it. It came out of her pocket, out of the pocket of her flowered apron. A piece of crumpled paper. A stiff lightly crumpled sheet of paper.

"Look," she said. "Just you look at this, an' you'll see."

So charged were her words that Superintendent Mouse, manoeuvring his huge bulk round in the direction of the Readers' Entrance and extending a ham fist in the direction of old Mr Lecroix's elbow, stopped and swung himself back round again.

"Look at what?" he demanded.

"Look at this piece o' paper what I picked up just under old Professor Grappelin's desk," Mrs Craggs said. "Get your old hornrims out, mate, and have a gander at this. Look, a piece of paper, stiff paper what's been wrapped round something. Ain't it? Ain't it?"

Superintendent Mouse, who, to do him justice, had ignored the word "mate" and had got out his hornrims and settled them across the bridge of his great squabby nose, peered and agreed.

"Yes. Stiff paper and wrapped round an object."

"An' you know why, don't you?" said Mrs Craggs. "Fingerprints. That's why. Well, if someone was keen to keep his fingerprints off of that there paperknife, it can only have been 'cos it wasn't the chap who owned the knife what used it. Everyone knew it was old Mr Lecroix's knife, so there wouldn't have been no point in him keeping his paw marks off it, would there? An', look, you can see the print o' that there cross handle on the paper, can't you? Can't you?"

Mr Tipton-Martin began to sidle very gently in the direction of the Readers' Entrance. But Superintendent Mouse, moving his great bulk with surprising speed, put it between him and the wide open spaces beyond. Then he looked at Mrs Craggs.

"It's Mrs — Mrs Craggs, isn't it?" he said. "Well, just give your full name and address to one of my officers, Mrs Craggs. I have a feeling we'll be needing you to give evidence sooner or later, and a witness who really knows what she's talking about is always a pleasure to have on hand."

And from old Mr Lecroix there came a murmured rider to that statement.

"Yes," he said, almost as if he was speaking to himself, "drink deep, or taste not the Pierian spring."

DICKER McLEISH'S GIRL

Ian Stuart

The boy was dimly aware of the sounds of traffic and a band. They seemed to come from a great distance, the skirl of pipes forming an obbligato to the rumble of cars and buses. Behind the great castle on its crag the sky was streaked with turquoise and gold, but here in the shadow of the trees it was already nearly dark. A minute, sixty short seconds before he had been free of all cares, triumphant, arrogant in his defiance, now suddenly he was afraid.

"Carole," he said, his thin, wheedling voice sharp with his fear. He repeated the name more urgently. "Carole!"

The girl didn't answer. He leaned over her, not understanding, knowing only that she was dead, yet hardly believing it.

"Oh Christ!" he breathed. And again, "Oh Christ!" The words tumbled out almost without his knowing, and perhaps they were a prayer rather than a blasphemy.

The cancer of fear was growing inside him, spreading outwards from its hard centre until it threatened to suffocate him. He could think of only one thing, that he must get away. From that place. From Edinburgh. To put as far as possible between himself and Dicker. He didn't know exactly what he had done, but the enormity of his crime and its inevitable consequences appalled him. Lowering the girl's head to the ground, he scrambled to his feet, his only thought to get away as quickly as he could.

He started running down the steep, winding path. A young couple were going down it and he pushed past, hardly seeing them as he jostled the girl, not hearing the boy's curse that followed him down. Hard asphalt jarred his feet through his plimsolls, but he was oblivious of the discomfort. Only his fear had any reality.

At the bottom of the path he stopped. To his left the road climbed round the side of the hill, heading eastwards towards the coast, and eventually, England. To his right it ran down to Princes Street where beyond the tower of the hotel the Scott Monument stood up, a shapely silhouette against the darkening sky. There was the city, the Old Town and the New. And that way lay danger.

The boy understood that. But it was the only world he knew, and like a frightened rabbit diving into its burrow he started running again, hardly noticing the car which came cruising up the road. There were two men in the car, Detective-sergeant Donald Smith and Detective-constable Kenneth McFadyen. McFadyen was driving.

"That's Andy McBain," he said. "He looks as if he'd seen a ghost."

Smith had already seen the boy. Crafty wee bastard, he thought.

McBain was a minor irritant, a hanger-on in the city's underworld, a world which at this time every year was swollen by half the pickpockets in England and a good many from the rest of Western Europe. Con men, too, looking for easy pickings among the tourists who gathered there from all over the world in search of culture and entertainment. A lad of seventeen already set on a life of petty crime.

Smith had nicked him a few weeks ago. Had him to rights. Then when it came to court McBain had produced witnesses he hadn't mentioned before and they had sworn he was with them when the shop was broken into. The sheriff had had some hard words for the police for not doing their work thoroughly. Which had meant Smith. And instead of keeping quiet and accepting that he was lucky, the boy had laughed in his face in front of his cronies and two young constables. Donny Smith wasn't the man to take treatment like that philosophically, and the sight of McBain's face now, haggard with fear, cheered him.

"I wonder what's scared him," he said softly.

"Shall we pick him up?" It had been a tedious evening so far, despite the festival, and McFadyen sounded hopeful.

"No, let's see what it was." Forty-three years old, the breadth of Smith's shoulders and the shortness of his neck made him look less than his five feet ten. He had the beginnings of a paunch, the result of many years' steady drinking, but he was tough, mentally and physically, and took pride in his toughness. A hard man, they called him. He knew it and gloried in it. He took an inverted pride too in the knowledge that he would never rise above his present rank. As if a man ceased to be quite a man if he became an inspector.

Together he and McFadyen strode up the path, meeting the couple almost at the bottom. They were wrapped up in each other, laughing and oblivious of the world.

The girl's body was lying a few feet from the path.

"Oh God!" McFadyen breathed, his voice shocked. "It's Dicker McLeish's girl."

Not Carole McLeish but Dicker McLeish's girl. Because at sixteen her only claim to recognition was her relationship to her father, his only child and the pride of his soul. In the unlikely event of Dicker having a soul. Half the city knew him or had heard of him, the small time gang boss, organiser of protection rackets, vice and half the crime in Edinburgh. Or so they said. Greengrocer, bully boy, extortioner, fence: Dicker McLeish. The hard yin.

"You get back to the car and report in," Smith said. He wanted time to think. "I'll stay here."

"What about the boy?" McFadyen asked.

"We can pick him up any time."

The constable stole another look at the crumpled form on the grass and walked away down the hill. The prospect of what Dicker would do when he heard the news horrified him.

When he had called in and reported what they had found he returned to where Smith was waiting.

"I'm going somewhere," the older man told him.

"But what about . . .?" McFadyen saw the sergeant's expression and stopped. He knew better than to argue with Smith when he was in his present mood. All the same, he was puzzled.

Smith told himself he had to hurry. He had about five minutes before the cars would arrive with the bright boys from headquarters, and if he wasn't back then they would want to know where he had been. In the meantime what they didn't know wouldn't hurt them.

Over the North Bridge Andy McBain slowed to an intermittent trot. He was panting and his legs ached. The pavement was crowded and people reacted angrily as he squirmed past, but he hardly noticed.

Save for an old derelict propped up against a shop's door the arcade was deserted. At the end McBain turned right into High Street. The band was no longer playing, but occasional sounds drifted down to him from the tattoo on Castle Esplanade. He was walking all the time now, his ebbing strength sapped by the slope, making for his room off Grassmarket. They would come looking for him there, he knew that as surely as he knew his own name, but it wouldn't be for a while yet.

He needed money. Without it he couldn't get away, and he was down to his last few pounds. That was no problem, he had plenty of friends who would help him, the only problem was time. He started running again, almost colliding with a man coming out of a pub half drunk.

"Wha's th' 'urry, Jimmy?" the man called after him. "Are the polis after you?"

McBain ignored him. There was a stitch in his side and his tortured body called out for respite, but he dared not stop. Up to Lawnmarket and down a steep alley dropping off the side of Castle Rock he went as fast as he could, sometimes stumbling with fatigue.

There were few people here among the narrow ways and crumbling tenements. Turning into a narrow close, he stopped at a door, glanced fearfully over his shoulder and, satisfied nobody was following him, pushed it open.

A woman's voice behind another door at the end of the passage called, "Who's that?"

"It's me, Mrs Campbell," the boy shouted back.

The old bag would be getting herself ready to go out for the evening, he thought. She might be a drab figure by day, but at night she blossomed out in the tawdry finery of a woman half her age. No use asking her for money, he owed a week's rent as it was, and she was as tight as an Aberdonian on a flag day. On weary legs he dragged himself up the stairs to his room on the third floor and threw himself down on the bed.

He had lived here for the last eight months, but for all the impression he had made on the dingy room it might have been a couple of weeks. True, there were a few photographs of nude girls cut out of magazines stuck on the walls with Sellotape, but they were nearly as impersonal as the ancient furniture.

After a few minutes the pain in his side eased and, pulling a shabby holdall down from the top of the wardrobe, he began cramming his few possessions into it. The task didn't take long, and when he had done he left, creeping down the stairs and out by the front door into the shadowy close.

Detective-inspector Logan watched Smith emerge from the darkness down the path. "Where have you been?" he demanded.

"I needed a quick leak," Smith told him.

Logan let it pass. He was thirty-eight, a lean, quietly spoken Highlander. He didn't like the other man, he hated his bully boy ways, his pride in his own macho image and his intolerance. Yet he knew that within his limitations Smith was a good policeman. He knew too that the dislike was mutual, that Smith despised him as soft, and that part of it was founded on envy, each seeing in the other a quality he would have liked to possess in some degree. With Logan it was the sergeant's assurance, even if it stemmed from the lack of perception which was one reason why he would never be promoted. Did Donny Smith ever wonder if he might be wrong? Logan doubted it.

"Has anything been touched?" he asked.

"I made sure she was dead," the sergeant replied in a voice as unyielding as a brick wall.

"Nothing else?"

"No, sir," McFadyen said.

The scene-of-crime officer and the photographer were at work.

"You say you saw a boy running away?" Logan enquired of McFadyen, resuming the questioning Smith's return had interrupted.

"Yes, sir, young Andy McBain. He looked scared."

"You know McBain, don't you, sergeant?" Logan was well aware of Smith's recent tribulations.

"I know him, aye."

"What do you know about him?"

"He's an errand boy for Dicker McLeish," Smith answered grudgingly. "He started taking the girl out and Dicker warned him to stay away from her."

"Carole was like the Holy Grail to Dicker," McFadyen volunteered.

Logan gave him a cynical look. "That pure?"

"In his eyes, sir. Maybe she was too."

"We'd better find the lad before he does then," Logan said.

"Aye," Smith agreed in his flat voice.

If you don't sound a bit less grudging, I'll have you back in uniform, Logan thought. But not just now. Not until I've squeezed all you know about this business out of you. "Where does McBain live?" he asked.

"He has a room wi' a Mrs Campbell near the Grassmarket," Smith said.

"You think he'll go there?"

"He may do. But no' for long, he'll know Dicker wull be after him."

Logan nodded. "I want a list of all his associates, anywhere he may go to ground. And a general call out for him. See to that, sergeant."

"Right," Smith said.

And show a bit more bloody enthusiasm. If only because there's a young constable listening and you're supposed to set him a good example, not use him as a shield because you know I won't bawl you out in front of him. "Now, sergeant."

"Yes, sir."

As McFadyen had done a short time before, Logan watched Smith's back disappear down the path and forced back the anger which had risen inside him like bile. Two men exchanged greetings in the darkness and a short elderly man in a raincoat and carrying a black bag emerged into the light.

"Evening, doctor," Logan said.

"Evening, inspector."

Their formality concealed a mutual liking and respect and Logan felt his irritation evaporating as he settled into the familiar routine of an investigation.

"Murder?" Doctor Laurie enquired, watching the scene-of-crime officer at work.

"Suspicious death until you tell us."

"Oh." The pathologist looked away through the darkness which concealed the lower slopes of the hill to the lights of the city. "Evenings are beginning to draw in, soon be autumn," he observed.

"And then winter, aye," Logan agreed.

"I havenae got twenty poonds just noo." Tommy Strachan looked uneasily at the queue beginning to form at his hot dog stand. Time wasted was custom lost, and this was by far his busiest time of the year. He had no intention of throwing away good money listening to Andy McBain. Anyway, he didn't like the look of it: Andy was one of Dicker McLeish's mob and he was scared.

To Strachan that spelt trouble. If Andy couldn't turn to Dicker for help, it must mean that the big man was the cause of his fear. And if he was, Tommy didn't want to know.

"I'll pay it back," McBain promised.

"Aye, maybe. Look, get awa' just noo, eh? I'm awful busy."

"Just ten then," Andy pleaded.

"Noo!"

You lousy, mean bastard, McBain thought. You wait till you need help and you come to me. But he knew when he was beaten, and he walked away down an alley which led by others equally narrow towards Canongate. Eddie Willis would be good for a tenner. Maybe twenty. He and Eddie were pals.

Coming out into High Street just below St Giles he looked furtively in both directions. What he saw stopped him in his tracks and brought his fear back as strong as ever. Thirty yards away on the other side of the street was a burly man with ginger hair growing low over his forehead. A man who looked as if violence was the only language he understood and who liked it that way. McBain knew him well.

For two or three seconds they stared at each other. Jamie McParland was one of McLeish's enforcers, among the first Dicker turned to when there was a reluctant publican or bookie to be persuaded. To McBain it seemed there could only be one reason for his being here now, and he felt sick with terror.

Then, without any sign that he had seen him, McParland spat into the gutter and walked away towards Lawnmarket.

It was the big man's failure to show any sign of recognition Andy found most frightening, and without looking back he took to his heels.

When he had gone a couple of hundred yards he turned left, then left again into another alley, stopping at a door set in the blank wall of a tenement. Its paint had ceased peeling long ago and only faint stains were left on the bare wood across which somebody had daubed "EDDIE'S INN" in crude red letters. Opening the door, he stepped inside.

The Inn was a cheap café, and most of its customers were under twenty-three. Some sported shabby leather jackets, others were in sweat shirts. There was a stench of cigarette smoke, cheap perfume, greasy food and bodies. A juke box against one wall blasted out a rock number.

A young man with lank dark hair and a heavy moustache which didn't suit his weedy frame was propping up the counter. When McBain walked in his expression, which had been bored, changed to alarm and he made an instinctive move towards the cupboard he called his kitchen. But there was no escape that way and he stopped.

The place was one of Andy's regular haunts, half the customers here now knew him, and he felt a faint spurious confidence returning.

"Hi, Eddie," he said.

"'Lo, Andy." Willis's apprehension was all too clear.

"I need twenty quid, Eddie. Urgent."

"Why come to me?"

"C'mon, Eddie. I'll pay you back next week."

"I cannae help you, Andy." Willis shot a frightened look at the nearest customers, as if he were afraid they might hear him. "I dinnae ken what you've done, but Dicker's put the word aboot. They're oot for you."

"I havenae done anything." The whining note had returned to the boy's tone. "I've got to get awa', Eddie. I'm skint, I must have twenty poonds."

"I cannae. I'm sorry, Andy."

McBain stared at him. Then, crushed by rejection and his own fear, he turned and slunk out.

"Doctor Laurie thinks she died of natural causes," Logan said. He noticed the flicker of aggression that passed briefly across Smith's rock-like features and wondered what it meant. Was it surprise? Relief that they weren't faced with a murder, or that Dicker wouldn't be spilling blood in his quest for revenge? Perhaps it meant nothing. "He can't find any signs of violence; it looks as if her heart just stopped beating. We'll have to wait for the results of the post mortem to know for sure, but it may have been quite a slight shock, he says. Some sort of inhibition. Possibly she had some congenital heart disorder."

"So why was McBain running away?" Smith demanded. "The next thing we hear, she wished herself dead."

"Maybe it was excitement," another man suggested. One or two of the others laughed.

Logan eyed Smith coolly. He knew now he'd been wrong, Smith wasn't glad Carole McLeish had died naturally, he'd wanted her death to be murder.

"What would you do if you found Dicker McLeish's daughter dead in your arms after he'd warned you to have nothing to do with her?" he wanted to know. "Would you go and tell him you were sorry but you didn't mean her to die? Would you, Smith? McBain must have believed he was responsible, and he's only a lad."

Logan told himself that Dicker no longer had any reason for hunting the boy. However unwilling he might be to accept it, Carole had died because of some failure of her own body. It was tragic, but not McBain's fault. And it wouldn't stop her father; McLeish wasn't a reasonable man.

It was nearly an hour since Logan had broken the news to him.

The inspector hated men like Dicker; with their greed and viciousness they almost justified the Donny Smiths, but he had felt sorry for the big man then. Yet he had had the feeling that while the grief was genuine, the shock wasn't new.

Logan had gone himself because he feared the consequences: when they were hurt the McLeishes of this world struck out blindly. Revenge was instinctive with them, and if Dicker knew that Carole was dead, he might also know that McBain had been with her.

"Has anybody come up with a sighting of the boy yet?" he asked. The other men shook their heads. "Is Dicker still at home?"

"Yes, sir," a uniformed sergeant said.

Logan wished he could share the sergeant's confidence. It was just a feeling, and perhaps he was being unduly pessimistic, but it was against nature for McLeish to sit at home nursing his grief and doing nothing.

"I want McBain found — fast," he said. "If he isn't, we may have a real murder on our hands." He was plagued by a nagging concern he couldn't put into words. He didn't believe in hunches or intuition, but there was a sense you acquired after long years in the job, and it was disturbing him now.

"McFadyen, go and see McLeish again," he said. "Don't harass him, just make sure he stays where he is."

Dicker had plenty of reserves he could call on to hunt down Andy McBain, all he had to do was lift his phone and speak to one of his lieutenants. Logan was pinning his hopes to a belief that this was something he would want to handle himself.

The other three men in the room watched Boxer Chisholm put down the phone.

"Where's he noo?" Dicker demanded.

"Eddie Willis says he's just been to his place begging for money," Boxer reported. "Eddie sent him awa'."

Dicker grunted. Getting out of his apartment over the shop had been as easy as kissing a baby. The copper who had been left to keep watch on the front didn't know he owned the adjoining apartment too, nor that there was a connecting door between them. All he'd had to do was slip through it, go down the stairs and out by the back door.

Now he was in no hurry. As long as the murdering wee bastard didn't leave Edinburgh, Dicker was happy for him to sweat a bit longer.

The phone rang again and the others waited while Chisholm went to answer it. This time the conversation was even briefer.

"That was Jamie," he said. "Andy's heading for Princes Street."

"He's going to see Queenie." An unpleasant smile spread slowly across McLeish's face. "Let's be going then, eh?"

On the esplanade a band was playing a quick march. McBain heard it as he descended the long flight of steps. Behind him the buildings rose sheer, a stone wall frowning down on the gardens, dark and menacing. Ahead were a wide expanse of turf and the Waverley Market with, beyond them, the lights of Princes Street. To his left, past the precipice of Castle Rock he could see the traffic moving up Lothian Road.

The music did nothing to lift his spirits. Fear obsessed him, so that he hardly noticed his aching legs or the thumping of his heart. Hope had deserted him, and he was almost resigned to what seemed the inevitable. He had seen more than one of the big man's victims after his thugs had dealt with them, their half-dead bodies bloodied and mutilated, and dully he wondered who Dicker would send for him.

Maybe he would come himself, to watch. Oh God!

"He's no' there," McFadyen reported, panting a little because he had run back to the car.

"Did you find out where he'd gone?" Logan demanded.

"No, sir. His woman's there, but all she'll say is that he went out a while ago. I don't think she knows."

"You'd better come back then." Logan replaced the phone. It was what he had feared.

Ten minutes ago a report had come in that McBain had been seen heading towards the Mound. There were policemen there; why, the whole force was grossly over-stretched coping with the

hordes of visitors and their problems. There was still some time
to go before the pubs closed, yet already this evening, in addition
to two pickpockets and a confidence trickster, a young Swede
had been stabbed in a brawl and there had been the usual quota
of drunks and thefts.

Logan walked across to the window and looked out. Here on
the north side of the city the festival made hardly any impression
on the quiet roads. But somewhere over there, a mile or two
away among the crowds, Andy McBain, scared out of his wits,
was running. Almost certainly McLeish was there too, bent on
revenge. Searching for them was like looking for two needles in a
haystack. Worse, the hay in this stack was continually shifting
and re-forming; it didn't stay still for a moment. Nor did the
needles. Yet in a way, Logan reflected, that might be an
advantage. A moving figure in the streets was more easily
spotted than one which remained indoors, and three cars were
cruising those streets now, their only object to find McBain
before McLeish did. The men in them knew the consequences of
failure. Logan went back to his desk and gave instructions for
McLeish to be brought in too.

When McFadyen returned, the inspector summoned him and
Smith.

"All right, let's go," he said. There was nothing more to be
gained by sitting waiting for other people to report success or
failure. He wanted to be out there, involved in what was going
on, and he could receive their reports in his car as well as here at
his desk.

The other two men followed him out to the yard. As the car
turned into the road the radio crackled.

"The boy's been seen at the end of Bank Street," McFadyen
reported. "It looks as if he's heading for Waverley Station."

Logan wondered if he hoped to lose himself in the crowds
there, or at that end of Princes Street. They said there was safety
in numbers and the best place to hide was in a crowd, but that was
true only when the crowd wasn't on the other side. Dicker
McLeish could call on a dozen, maybe twenty toughs and back
street informants, while Andy McBain was on his own. There
was little enough safety in odds like those.

On the other hand, there were plenty of places to hide around a big station and it would take a major operation to flush him out if he went to ground there. Logan thought it unlikely he intended to take a train, a boy like him would be more likely to hitch a lift on a lorry, preferably one going a long way.

"Where do you reckon he's making for?" Logan asked Smith, who was sitting in the back of the car alone, looking out of the window apparently unconcerned. Barely even interested. His lack of involvement irritated Logan anew.

"He could be going to Queenie Henderson's," the sergeant suggested. Mrs Henderson ran a cheap café and lodging house frequented by the likes of McBain and his friends.

"It's a fair way if he is, and he's been on the run for the best part of two hours already," Logan commented.

Smith said nothing.

The car swung round the end of Princes Street into a square, momentarily leaving the bright lights and the crowds behind. Then they were round the other side and back on Princes Street heading east, the siren wailing now as they weaved in and out of the lines of slow-moving traffic.

Dicker saw McBain when he was near the end of Market Street. The big man hadn't run more than a dozen yards at a stretch for years, but he ran now, ignoring his thudding heart and the stitch in his side. His henchmen lumbered in his wake.

McBain heard their heavy footsteps behind him and looked back over his shoulder. There were four of them, Dicker and three others. He knew them all. Driving his exhausted limbs on desperately, he made for the south end of Waverley Bridge. A police car's siren wailed somewhere ahead of him, but the sound was too familiar and his fear too real for him to pay any attention to it. It didn't occur to him that it might represent safety, the police were as much his enemies as McLeish and his toughs.

Three men were running towards him from the other end of the bridge. In the half light, his eyes bleary with fatigue and sweat, he didn't recognise them, but he knew they must be three more of Dicker's mob. McLeish was only fifty yards behind him now and sobbing, desperate, he swerved to his left. Straight for the parapet of the bridge.

There was no one to pull him back. Those people near enough were too startled to move. They watched, horrified, as he scrambled up on to the low wall and stood there, silhouetted against the lights of Princes Street behind him.

"McBain, stop! We are the police," Logan shouted.

He was too late. Or perhaps the boy didn't hear him. In any case, he believed he had as much to fear from the law as from his old associates. For a second or two he balanced there and it seemed to Logan that time stood still, then he fell.

His thin scream was lost in the sound of the train coming out of the station.

Logan had sent McFadyen out of the room and now he and Smith were alone. The inspector knew that if he allowed full rein to the anger and bitterness he felt, he would lose control of the situation and the sergeant's only reaction would be contempt. He intended every word he spoke to pierce the older man's thick, complacent skin. If either of them was to lose his cool, it must be Smith. So he waited before he said, "I'll give you the benefit of the doubt and assume you didn't mean young McBain to be killed." He spoke slowly and his tone had an edge like a knife's.

"You'll — " Smith began contemptuously.

"Wait until I've finished, sergeant." It came out like a whiplash. "I say I'll assume you didn't expect McLeish to kill McBain when you told him you'd found his daughter dead and the boy running away. You just wanted him roughed up. To teach him a lesson for making you look a prat. You knew what his daughter meant to Dicker, and you saw a way of paying McBain back and doing McLeish for g.b.h. at the same time."

"What makes you think I told him?" Smith had spoken coolly, almost insolently, but a pulse was throbbing in his forehead.

"I don't think, sergeant. I know. You found her within a minute or two of the boy running away. Nobody went up that path ahead of you and nobody came down except the couple you met. They were only interested in each other. After you found her there was somebody on guard there the whole time and no outsider went near her. Yet when I went to tell Dicker what had happened he already knew. You didn't go to relieve yourself, sergeant, you went to phone him from the box at the bottom of the path."

Their eyes met.

"Is this official — sir?" Smith demanded.

Logan regarded him coldly. He wanted Smith to see the contempt he felt. "No," he said. "It isn't official, sergeant. I can't prove it. But I know what happened. I won't have you working with me again — ever. And if I find you stepping out of line, in any way, you'll pay for it. In full. Now get out."

For a second it seemed that Smith was going to say something, but he turned and went out of the room without speaking.

TWO OF A KIND

Herbert Harris

Paul smiled fondly at the girl across the table, his look containing more of pride than desire.

Not that he was entirely past the age of eager passions — fifty was not old nowadays, was it? — but this cool, placid blonde, despite her siren qualities, was plainly not promiscuous.

"More champagne, Nikki?" But the shiny gold hair moved springily as she shook her head.

"You deserve it," he told her appreciatively. His smile made crow's-feet between his eyes and greying temple hair. She returned a half-smile and shook her head again.

He regarded her speculatively as he lit a cigar. She had class, this one, an inbuilt elegance. Her simple white dress fitted superbly. Her hair, her make-up revealed a gift for subtlety.

But there was a coldness, a lack of compromise in the high cheeks, the straight pointed nose. Just as well. She wasn't likely to let female emotions get in the way of business.

"Your young baronet was a useful find, Nikki. You did well bringing him to the sacrificial altar. Poor lad," he added with an ironic grin.

"You needn't feel sorry for him," she answered. "He's stinkingly rich. He could lose ten times what he lost without batting an eyelid."

"Could we take him on another trip?"

"No!" Her response was sharp, decisive. "We made it a rule that lightning should never strike twice in the same place. You said yourself it could draw too much attention to us."

He nodded. She had a good head, he thought. No nonsense. No silly chances. Not just beautiful, but damned smart. In time she would make a full-fledged partner of real talent.

He had been lucky to recruit her. If he hadn't gone to the Golden Dice Club that night, he would never have met her. And within half-an-hour of their meeting, he had known she was what he had been looking for. Her poise was unusual for one so young, her mind razor-sharp, her sex appeal devastating and yet somehow dispassionate.

Because she was so exactly right, he was overjoyed when she showed interest in his proposition. Then, when she had at last thrown in her lot with him, he had been able to teach her in an astonishingly short time the arts and wiles of card-sharping.

"Even ordinary poker, played legitimately, calls for a high degree of intelligence — it's more than a battle of wits, it's a clash of personalities," he had expounded with enthusiasm, "and the kind *we* shall play, Nikki, will be even more fascinating . . . and more deadly!"

Paul, a gambler for thirty years, was the complete "pro" at the card-table, even when his game was not "bent". But sharping was a challenge. And who could ever shout "Swindler!" at this cultured man with the gently twinkling eyes, greying hair, and quiet confidence of a company chairman?

Nikki was now "my daughter", and Paul was "Daddy". They made a handsome, even inspiring pair.

Now it was the cool blonde who managed — finally — to have the astounding run of luck at the card-table.

"Finally" being the operative word. At first the human sacrifice had to have all the luck. And how cocky these sacrificial lambs could get, how flushed with success, how reckless, before the others moved in. . . .

"It's positively flukey how my daughter manages to win in the end!" — a paternally indulgent chuckle from Paul.

And from Nikki, the spoiled daughter with the Midas touch: "I carry a lucky charm, you see! It's brought me luck everywhere, even at Monte Carlo!" Lucky charm indeed — not a wrong call or faulty "raise" for quite a while. . . .

Beautiful, Paul mused, beautiful. He drained the rest of the champagne and looked at her hopefully.

"Of course, you have someone else lined up?"

She gave him a businesslike nod, leaning across the table so that the valley deepened between her breasts. Yes, he decided, she'd be a great asset in trapping victims for skinning. . . .

"Not a baronet this time. No title at all. Just the over-subsidised son of a rich papa."

"Excellent. When?"

"You're the boss," she told him. "It's for you to decide the time and place. I just supply the innocent."

Ronnie Doyle was the archetypal innocent lamb.

Tall, fair-haired, almost gangling in his schoolboyishness. A clear pink skin, smooth as if he had only just begun shaving. His slight stutter became worse when Nikki stroked his hand.

"This one's straight from the cradle," Paul whispered while Doyle was momentarily out of earshot.

"A gold-plated cradle," Nikki whispered back. "Don't worry — he's actually twenty-one."

Doyle hadn't been to the Golden Dice Club before, and was fascinated by the old-world Regency atmosphere, the luxurious setting in which a budding buck could blossom.

"You can play anything here," Paul said. "Roulette, chemmy, baccarat, stud poker, blackjack, pontoon, Las Vegas dice, the lot . . . but give me poker every time. A game that exercises the grey matter, like bridge or chess. You play?"

"Of course he does, Daddy!" Nikki put in, sounding hurt. "You played at college, didn't you, Ronnie?"

And so, at one of the small exclusive tables which Paul saw as a kind of surgeon's operating-table, they began to play.

It should have been a long game, running maybe to 150 hands by the finish. But it ended with a shattering suddenness halfway through, just when Ronnie Doyle had built up a massive accumulation of chips.

"T-t-tonight," Doyle had stammered excitedly, "I think I shall m-make my f-fortune!"

"Good for you!" Paul had smiled, his smile less expansive than usual. If his mouth had a firmer set, it was because the stakes had mounted too dizzily, and he had parted with a lot more than he normally considered safe.

But not to worry. They would get it all back, and more. The suckling babe would wonder what had hit him. . . .

Then, suddenly, Nikki's golden head was lowered and she was pinching the bridge of her nose. "I . . . I'm afraid I'm feeling faint," she said in a low voice.

She swayed first, then toppled sideways like a felled tree in Doyle's direction. The young man broke her fall, holding her by her shoulders.

"We'd better get her home!" Doyle said.

Paul swallowed, his face grim. Christ, what a time to flake out! "She'll be all right in a few minutes," he said. "I'm sure she'd like to play on a bit longer. . . . "

The young man frowned disapprovingly. "It's not important, is it? Another night perhaps. The thing now is to get her home!"

His solicitude suggested that this callow youth might have fallen for Nikki. God forbid that she had fallen for *him*!

She surely wouldn't have conned him out of a few lousy grand to help this babe-in-arms out of a jam or anything? She could have asked, couldn't she? But, no, that was something she could never do — actually *ask*. . . .

Next day she told him as much, her face still enamelled in its cold calmness and bland indifference.

"I'm very like my father," she told him. "He was proud, too. He could never crawl to anyone, never ask favours. You might remember him. My real surname, by the way, is Kilbride — that was my father's name."

"Kilbride?" Paul repeated, dredging his memory. "You mean . . . David Kilbride?"

"So you do remember?"

"Yes, I remember — it must be two years ago."

"You took him for a lot more than he could afford," Nikki said. "He stole from his firm to cover his losses and they fired him. He's been living rather frugally since then."

"I see." He stared at her. "So this is revenge, is it?"

"And one way of getting back the money you cheated my father out of."

"How much do you have to pay the young gigolo?"

"Nothing. His name's Kilbride too. He's my brother."

Paul shook his head sadly. "I'll miss you," he told her sincerely. "You were magnificent while it lasted."

He tried to stare her out, but the ice-blue eyes never wavered. He glanced at his watch. "I'll have to fly," he said. "After all, I shall be busy looking for a replacement."

She didn't answer. His last glimpse was of an almost too-perfect blonde wearing something like a Mona Lisa smile. And once away from her, he shrugged fatalistically.

After all, he was a gambler. One had to lose sometimes. But there was one thing that left a lingering bitter taste.

He hadn't "sharped" in that game with David Kilbride. He had won all the hands "dead straight" — one of the few completely straight games he had ever played.

THE STAIRS OF SAND

Peter Godfrey

"*William Simmons?*"

"*Yes, sir.*"

"*You will kindly address your replies not to me, but to his Lordship. Now: your name is William Simmons?*"

"*Yes, my Lord.*"

"*You are charged with the crime of murder, in that on the night of August 12, 2088, at Esher, in the county of Surrey, you wilfully killed by strangulation one Joseph Dexter. How do you plead — guilty or not guilty?*"

"*Guilty, my Lord.*"

What did they expect me to say? I killed Dexter, didn't I? That's the plain physical fact. My fingers gripped his throat, iron entered my muscles, my hate and fear galvanised my strength, and he was dead.

Guilty, my Lord! That's all I can tell the law, and all that the law really wants to know.

So many things have deteriorated, you see. Almost everything.

Nor is it hard to isolate the reason for this. I'm not quoting from my own experience, you must understand — that would be too arrogant. None of this reasoning arises out of my own memory, which is notoriously non-existent. Recently, though, I've studied the history books and come to my own conclusions.

I think the basic start of this cultural regression was the discovery that human life could not exist in the cosmos beyond a few thousand miles from Earth itself, because space ships had continually to be refuelled and revictualled.

The realisation was a great shock to humanity. War had been

abolished for so long and the population explosion so great that humanity suddenly found itself face to face with its greatest crisis in a long history of crises.

So, in a series of carefully calculated measures, the World Government deliberately took steps to defederate itself. At the same time, all over the world the massive propaganda machines strained themselves to stimulate new regional patriotism. Old idealism and old grudges burst into flame. One last solemn international agreement was entered into to ban nuclear, bacteriological, and certain chemical weapons, and then the war to start wars again was allowed to commence.

On both sides, all the propaganda emphasis was directed approvingly to a virtue that had not been thought about for many generations — courage. The hero became an idealised figure; the coward was scorned and detested by all.

When we went back to war, all our culture seemed somehow to slip back in time, too. As children in school, learning history, we used to laugh at the uncivilised attitudes of the imperial patriots — now, suddenly, we all became super-jingos ourselves. And despite the horrors of the new war, some of it carried on after the armistice was signed.

Tastes changed. There was an overt groping on the video scene toward romantic and violent plays. These usually took the form of historical tales. The playwright Shakespeare was the most popular, perhaps because he was so imaginative and versatile. And he was easy to produce, too.

Likewise, the law itself changed. Old shibboleths like extenuating circumstances, psychological stress, and rehabilitation were too closely and uncomfortably associated with similar liberal sentiments which had been reviled during the war as cowardice. As a consequence, the law began to move away from humanitarianism and toward revengeful punishment. Someone has been killed and so someone must be put to death in retaliation. An eye for an eye, and a tooth for a tooth.

But whatever people say, I know, just because I am guilty, that there are things even more important than the physical facts.

The gleam in Dexter's eye, for instance, when he spoke about the Heroes Clubs. "I can't understand you, Simmons. All over the world, in the smallest villages as well as the cities and towns, clubs are being formed. You yourself say all your friends are joining, yet you still hang back. Why?"

"I don't know. There's something — I can't quite give it a name. That's why I'm here. I thought perhaps if I spoke to you, the leader and originator of the movement, I might overcome this doubt."

"What do you want to know?"

"About the ultimate aims of the movement. Not what appears in the brochures, but what you yourself feel."

His expression was half puzzled, half flattered. I could see his eyes trying to read the emotions behind the disfiguring scar on my face. "I still don't understand," he said. "After all, you went through the war."

"Perhaps it's because of the war that I'm doubtful."

He shrugged. "Well, what can I tell you? The Heroes Clubs are, as their name implies, clubs for heroes."

"I'm no hero."

"Of course you are. Any man who saw action is a hero. I think I know your trouble now, Simmons. You've come back from all that hell, seen all the promises made to you go up in smoke, and now you're so disillusioned you're not prepared to believe anything. Join up with us, man — and help."

I said: "I'm a member of an ex-servicemen's organisation, the Corps. In what way is your movement superior?"

"In every way. Like you, we keep alive the comradeship of the slit trench, the brotherhood under a hail of life-threats. But in every way we go further. You help the ex-serviceman by lending him money, petitioning higher authority, and so on. In other words, you *ask* for favours. We in the Heroes Clubs *demand* our rights."

I tried to bring him down to earth. "That's theoretical quibbling. What different methods can you use in practice?"

The light in his eye was wild. "We fought in the war in order to change the world — and the battle is not yet over for us. We, those who earned the right to be considered a new aristocracy through bloodshed and pain endured, why shouldn't we control the countries we fought for?"

I said: "The war took something from all of us. How can you be sure it left us fit to govern?"

"Because in this shattered world we're the cream — and cream always rises to the top."

"So does scum."

His face suddenly purpled.

I went on: "So what is your plan? Are you starting a new political party?"

"No!" He almost spat out the word — and then, suddenly, laughed. "I told you we are different. All this trumpery of government and democracy is designed only to impress fools, and to keep power out of the hands of those who deserve to rule. But that situation will soon be reversed. How? I'll tell you, my friend. By two powerful factors — leadership and organisation. I am the leader, and the organisation is now nearly complete."

He peered into my face again as though trying to read my thoughts. "In every country of the world there are Heroes Clubs. Our total membership is colossal — and for every hundred members we have thousands of friends and sympathisers. When the time comes, in every centre of population on the globe the Clubs will simply march in and take over the machinery of government. Nobody will want to do anything about it. Even the armed forces will be on our side. I'll give a word of command, and in a few hours the old order will disappear and the new era will be firmly in control."

It was strange he should talk so frankly. I had the feeling that somehow my disfigured lack of expression had egged him on.

"I see," I said. "You're aiming at revolution. And what sort of society will you set up? The ordinary civilians who also made their wartime sacrifices, what will be their relationship with your new aristocracy?"

"I'll proceed on the principle that he who isn't for us is our enemy. But that's only a theoretical conception — there will be no opposition. As for how I will rule, I will rule as the military machine rules, my friend — by edict. I'll give an order, and three hundred million followers will spring to attention and obey. Can you imagine what that will mean for the world? Rule by efficiency, no bureaucratic delays, no vacillating debates — one command, and what is possible to be done will be done."

I burst out then: "Of course there'll be opposition! Do you really think the men who went through all those horrors and returned with a deep perception of themselves as individuals will allow themselves to become puppets again? Follow you blindly into an international dictatorship? Do you imagine they'll be bluffed indefinitely by the pseudo-idealism under which you cloak your lust for power?"

Again he laughed. "I see I've misjudged you, Simmons. But I'm not afraid of you, or of all the other cowards and pacifists in the world. Even if you started organising against me tonight and everyone believed you, you wouldn't be nearly ready as an effective opposition by the time I order the takeover."

It was his confidence more than anything that provoked the feeling of desperation in me. "And if you do gain power," I said, "what then? Do you think we cowards and pacifists, as you call us, will simply leave it at that?"

"That contingency has been considered," he said. "After I've gained power, there will be no more cowards and pacifists."

I gasped. "Do I understand that as leader of the Heroes Clubs, you would order the extermination of all those whose sentiments might prejudice your position?"

"That is correct."

"Then you will never give that order, Dexter," I said.

"And after you heard the noise, Mrs Dexter, what did you do?"
"I took my husband's pistol and came down the stairs."
"What did you see?"
"The accused was bending over my husband's body."
"You spoke to him?"
"Yes. I asked him what had happened."
"And he replied?"
"That he had killed my husband."
"Then what did you do?"
"I detained him with the pistol while I telephoned the police."

When I looked up, it was the pistol I saw first, a gleaming mouth

ready to spit death. Then I became conscious of the human
being holding it.

There was a large vase of flowers on the table at the foot of
the stairs, and the wallpaper had a rose-cluster pattern. Her
black négligée was almost indistinguishable from the shadows
and the flower motif momentarily camouflaged her pale face
with the red slash of her lips. Perhaps that was why I saw the
pistol first, or perhaps it was because the kind of death I fear
most is a bullet searing through my flesh.

There was a long pause after I told her I had killed her
husband. At least it seemed long to me, because there appeared
to be no reason for it. Then it occurred to me that she must hate
me, that she might be contemplating shooting me. In a flash of
panic I cried out: "Why don't you call the police?"

Her voice shook, but her hand was steady. "First there is
something I must know. Why did you do it?"

"Because of the Heroes Clubs," I told her.

Her eyes narrowed with pain. "Judas Iscariot!" she said.

Did her finger whiten on the trigger?

"Don't shoot!" I said wildly.

"No, not Judas. You're too much of a coward even for that."
Then she broke out fiercely. "Oh you *fool*! If you'd killed him
for any of a dozen reasons — his cruelty, his intolerance, his
fear of being hurt — but to murder him for the one decent thing
he'd applied his energy to since the war, the one thing that
made me see in him something of the man I thought I'd
married!"

"Decent!" I said bitterly. "Is that what you call his scheme of
enslavement? Was his megalomania the quality you admired?
Was it your ambition to be the power behind the throne of the
Emperor of the World?"

She stared at me. "Is that the interpretation you put on the
Heroes Clubs? You idiot, can't you realise my husband was
working for a great ideal, without any thought of himself? Oh,
the war was cruel to him, I'll admit, but it wasn't for any motive
of revenge that he started the movement. It was because he felt
that the men who had suffered could best ensure that there
would be no more suffering."

I said: "I'm one of those who suffered. If that had been his motive, I'd have been his most devoted follower. But all he wanted was personal power. Did you know he was prepared to exterminate anyone who opposed his views?"

"I don't believe it."

"It's true, nevertheless. I saw him tonight for what he is — a monster prepared to wade through human blood to perpetuate power."

"And that's why you killed him?"

"That's why I killed him."

There was a pause, then: "I don't know why I talk to you," she said.

I knew, though. It was to convince herself of the untruth of the doubt I had raised in her mind.

She went on: "You remember before the war how famous Joe Dexter was? There was hardly a week between the stories of his exploits in the newspapers. His car and plane racing, his Amazon exploration, his mountain-climbing and big-game triumphs. I was a schoolgirl then, and like so many others I made Joe something of a personal hero, although I'd never met him.

"Then one night he gave a lecture in our town. I've heard it said that when you worship from afar you're always disappointed on closer contact. But it wasn't that way with Joe. He had a vibrancy that pictures and articles didn't show and my imagination hadn't supplied. Little things. Like an unconscious gesture he had of crooking the fingers of his right hand and running the thumb over the fingertips. It was a gesture so gentle, yet so full of resolve.

"That night, though I didn't actually meet him, I stopped worshipping him like a schoolgirl and began to love him as a woman.

"The next time I saw him was years later, when I was a nurse at a military hospital near Darwin, Australia. I wouldn't have known it was Joe if it hadn't been for his identification tag. The first time I undid the bandages round his head, I tensed myself for the shock of the disfiguring wound, but I was still not prepared for the featureless bloody mask that met my eyes. That gesture, too, that had thrilled me so had been left behind on the battlefield with his right arm.

"He lay there for months, mostly unconscious, barely living, but I had several photographs of him and the surgeon was interested in his case. After the seventeenth operation, his face was as you knew it — less mobile and expressive than before but identical, feature for feature.

"We were married three days after his discharge. Then I found that what the surgeon had done for him hadn't been enough. The surgery he needed most was to his mind.

"He was taciturn — abnormally so. His every action was mean and vindictive. And then one day when we were out together, a savage dog attacked us. He gave a whimper of fear and thrust me as a shield between the animal and himself." Her voice was charged with emotion. "I should have left him then. Afterward, though, when he started to organise the Heroes Clubs, I was glad I'd hung back.

"Not that it made any difference in his treatment of me. He seemed to disregard me more and more. Sometimes I was a chattel to be used, when he had guests another ornament in his house, never a woman to whom he could pour out his dream. But I saw the dream clearly, for all that. I saw it in his concentration, in his quicker movements, in the set of his jaw, in the light in his eyes when he spoke about the Clubs."

"You saw something in him of the man you first knew?"

"No," she said, "don't misunderstand me. He wasn't the same. There had been a charm about him before — but the war killed that. It just seemed to me that in this new energy he had found a weapon against his memory of the war, a weapon of revenge for him and for me."

I said: "No, you're wrong. All he felt was a lust for power."

"When you think of the war," she asked suddenly, "what emotion do you feel?"

"Horror," I said. "I smell the death and feel as though at any moment there can be searing pain — and something tugging at my muscles, trying to force me to run."

There was triumph in her voice. "I knew it — you're a coward. But he had something inside him even the war couldn't kill. Something that forced him to be a fighter to the last."

I stood silent, conscious only of the muzzle of the pistol, the life pulsing in my veins, the death at my feet.

She said, "I don't know why I want you to understand, but I do. I want you to realise what he was fighting. War, yes, and what war can do. Think back on actual incidents — shellfire, dive-bombers coming at you, perhaps — anything that actually happened to you in those days. Do you remember?" She paused, waiting for my answer, ready to draw from it her moral, a logical conclusion.

"Remember? No," I said. "No, I don't remember."

"You are a mental specialist, Dr Andrews?"

"A psychoneurologist — yes."

"Under what circumstances did you meet the accused?"

"I treated him as a patient in Kookaburra Military Hospital and later I attended him privately in this country after his discharge."

"What was the nature of his illness?"

"Amnesia — loss of memory."

"When did you cease treatment?"

"On May fifth of this year."

"That was approximately three months before the murder. Was the accused cured?"

"No. I'd done everything I could without getting results. I told him that his cure could be a matter of chance. Some casual incident or scene might suffice to bring his memory back."

"Have you examined the accused since the murder?"

"Yes, three days ago."

"And you came to what conclusion?"

"That he is still suffering from amnesia."

Coming home — only I didn't recognise it as home. Strange place, strange people. A visitor, not a returning son.

Vividly conscious that I was William Simmons, corporal, of Weybridge, Surrey, who joined the King's Twelfth Infantry in Guildford in 2081, fought in Malaysia and Australia, twice wounded — but conscious of it not as a memory, but as information typed for me from military papers and read over and over again. Not a prominent citizen, anyway, or someone would have recognised me despite the scar. Unknown, unwanted, a stranger, with a great loneliness and a mysterious sense of loss.

Looking through the records once again, there I am — William Simmons, born November 14, 2059. Father dead, mother dead, no other family. The place where I'd once lived blasted clean off the earth and now the site of an imposing block of luxury apartments. A nobody returning to nothing.

Then finding companionship in the Corps, building a new life and new friendships with all those others who had been lucky enough to return from the war. Looking forward all week to the Thursday-night gatherings, the cheerful conversation. Living again.

"Those Aussie kids in Canberra — remember how they used to beg for food?"

"God, that dust! Remember when there wasn't enough water how the boys all used to dream of cold beer?"

I lied. I said I remembered.

Then all the happiness shattered, so quickly, so insidiously. Men coming in saying, "I won't be in next Thursday, I've joined the Heroes Club." First one or two, then more and more, until finally there were only three left in the Corps.

"Why don't you join up, too, Bill? What's your objection?"

I had no logical motive, just an unreasoning unease, and the fear, not of present pain, but of being hurt in the future.

Then Dexter arrived on the scene.

"In amnesia cases, Dr Andrews, does the patient forget every-thing? Does he lose the faculty of remembering incidents that occur after the onset of illness?"

"No. This type of amnesia does not involve actual brain damage. The illness is caused by psychological shock. The patient does not recall details of the shock or anything prior to that shock, but he will remember subsequent events clearly."

"So that an amnesia sufferer can still weigh up conflicting arguments, decide right from wrong?"

"Yes."

"In other words, in the present case, if the accused suffered the primary psychological shock prior to the murder, at the time of the

crime he would be quite competent to realise the implications of what he was doing?"

"Yes."

"And in point of fact the accused did *suffer that primary shock long before the murder?*"

"Yes. He was reported as an amnesia case in Kookaburra in March, 2086."

Australia, March 2086, Hospital. Dull ache in the back, burning pain in the face. Thick lips mumbling through bandages, "Doctor, can't we try again?"

"Don't be impatient, Simmons. It'll come to you eventually. Now — did you dream last night?"

"Yes."

"Tell me about it."

"I was in a garden and wanted to dig. I looked around for a spade, but there was only a broken piece of handle stuck in the ground. Just then a bee came buzzing up. I thought it was going to sting me and ran for the house. The door was locked and when I banged on it it suddenly changed to heavy black curtains. They fell over my head and I woke up."

"How do you feel about that dream, Simmons? Was it pleasant or unpleasant to you?"

"Very unpleasant, sir."

"Oh? Well, let's see if you can remember exactly what emotions were roused in you by the different elements of the dream. The garden?"

"Only the feeling that I had a duty to dig."

"The broken spade?"

"A sort of relief, sir — as though I was rather glad I didn't have to dig at all."

"The bee?"

"Fear."

"The locked door?"

"A sense of frustration."

"The curtains falling over your head?"

"That was horrible, sir. *They were velvet, and they — choked.*"

*

"Feeling better this morning, Simmons?"

"Yes, sir."

"Well, let's discover how much you've progressed. Think back. What's your earliest memory?"

"Lying in this bed."

"There must be something before that."

"No. Yes. The feel of the sheets."

"And even before that?"

"Nothing, sir. Just black."

"What kind of black? A dark night?"

"No, sir. More solid. Like a curtain — a heavy velvet curtain."

"You can feel it with your hands?"

"Yes."

"Right. Now keep your eyes closed, Simmons — and concentrate hard. It's only a curtain, understand? Just a harmless length of cloth. So, push! Push it aside with your arms and walk through."

"I can't. There are too many folds. *They're falling over my face!*"

"It's only a curtain, Simmons, only a curtain. *Push.* Do you hear me? Force yourself through!"

"Oh, my God! I'm smothering!"

"Let's try some word association. You don't have to think for this. I say a word and you tell me the first word that comes into your mind. Ready?"

"Yes, sir."

"All right. Cat?"

"Dog."

"Dog?"

"Fight."

"Fight?"

"Dig."

"Dig?"

"Bee."

"Bee?"

"Run."

"Run?"

"Door."

"Door?"

"Curtain."

"Curtain?"

"Oh, no, sir, no!"

"William Simmons, you have pleaded guilty, and on the evidence before me this court must accept your plea as correct without the slightest hesitation. There remains, then, only the possibility of extenuating circumstances.

"Your defence counsel has argued that your amnesia indicates a lack of mental balance. This contention has been rebutted by the prosecution. The only concern of the law is whether, at the moment of the commission of the crime, the accused knows what he is doing and is able to assess the consequences of his action. This court has no doubt you were mentally competent at the time of your crime.

"In your own evidence, you alleged your motive was political, that the deceased was plotting a form of revolution. In the absence of any corroborative evidence, this court cannot believe that story. Not only did the deceased have a fine military record, but his entire career seems to have been based on patriotism coupled with humanitarian missions in no way consistent with the motives ascribed to him by you.

"But even if the court was disposed to believe your story, it could not accept that motive as an extenuating circumstance. Murder can never be considered a justifiable method of removing political differences.

"Although there may be some doubt as to your real motive, the physical facts of the case are perfectly clear. They are that on the night of August twelfth of last year, being at the time sound of mind and body, you attacked and strangled to death a one-armed and defenceless man — a crime which can only be described as brutal and cowardly. It is therefore the sentence of this court that you be taken from here to the place from whence you came — "

And from there to this place, to hang by the neck until I'm dead.

Three weeks ago he said it, and I can still hear his voice: "At a time and place to be appointed." This place. Tomorrow.

For a brutal and cowardly crime.

Am I really a coward? The judge thinks so, *she* thinks so, the world thinks so. But what do I think?

If you take the physical facts, as the judge did, as she did, then I am. But isn't there something over and above the physical facts?

Let me take stock of myself. Repentance? No, I'm not sorry I killed Dexter. I think if I could relive it and all that's happened since, I'd do it again. Fear? I don't think so. My mind doesn't dwell on tomorrow.

Or perhaps I don't think of tomorrow because I *am* afraid?

Well, there's one way to judge. Imagine. They come for me. The straps tighten around my arms. The strangling noose — Yes, I am afraid.

But does fear necessarily indicate cowardice? Is a man brave because he feels no fear, or because he persists in a course of action despite fear? The torture is that I can't decide. If only I knew what kind of man I was before the amnesia, what my ambitions were, what emotions I'd experienced, then perhaps I could judge.

"Simmons!"

"Yes, warder?"

"The chaplain is outside. Won't you see him today, old man?"

"No. I don't want to see him."

"Okay. Sorry I interrupted your concentration."

"How did you know I was concentrating?"

"By your habit."

"My habit?"

"Yes. The way you bend your right hand and run your thumb over the tips of your fingers."

In a vivid mental flash, I saw her again, behind the gun. I heard her voice. "So typical, that gesture." The words came loud and clear, yet somehow they seemed very far away. The folds of the dark curtain were about me, not choking this time, but pulling aside, metre upon metre of it, swifter and swifter, so that the nap of the velvet on my face sent tiny shocks up my spine. Then the curtain was gone, and I was on the other side.

I was Joe Dexter, and I was sharing a shellhole with a man who gibbered and scrabbled with frenzied fingers to dig himself deeper and deeper into the mud. He was mad with fear. I think it was the Helli that did it. We had gone for so long without meeting those sharks of the sky that the sudden appearance of this one was a dreadful shock. Its zooming buzz over the crump of the shells seemed to be the last straw for him.

Twice I had to hit him to keep him from running into the open, and each time the desperation of the blows helped allay the rising tide of panic within me. Then, just as I thought he was going to lie quiet, he twisted from my grasp and ran.

Not far, though. A mortar shell got him, and tore off his face and his right arm, blew him out of his clothes, and hurled his body back into the shellhole.

And the faceless thing he now was was still unconscious, still gibbered, still scrabbled with its remaining fingers into the dirt.

I, too, went mad then. By a strange mental paradox, I accepted the terror of the moment. It was what the future might hold that cut my soul like a knife. In one second, a thousand memories buffeted my mind. I smelled the fetid smell of the Amazon undergrowth, flinched from the unexpected hissing snarl of a jaguar, felt the wind from the rhino's horn as it charged me at Serengeti, knew the fragmentation of my nerves as my car smashed through the race-track barrier, saw the screaming headlines, heard again the sandy-haired little man on the bus say: "What will this fellow Dexter do next?"

I saw the future then, the war over, but peace bringing a thousand new perils I'd have to face just because I was Joe Dexter and that is what my public would expect of me. And I saw each picture individually, and I lived how I would feel — with terror rasping my spine, and overtaxed nerves shivering for peace.

I thought of the peace that only death could provide. But when I thought of death, a greater fear, like cold feathers, whirled inside me.

I thought, Why shouldn't he be Joe Dexter?

And the idea prompted my muscles before it reached my mind. I found I had already torn off my uniform and my right hand was bleeding from the force with which I'd wrenched off my wrist-chain and identity disc. I knelt down to do the same to the half man lying there before realisation froze me. His arm — it was gone. I'd forgotten that.

I crawled out, hugging the ground until I reached the new crater. I searched round the centre, up the sides, the edges. Then the odds against finding what I sought in the dark struck me suddenly like a blow. But as it did, there was a flash from a nearby explosion and I saw a wrist with extended fingers protruding from the dirt. I gripped it like the hand of a long-absent friend and the arm pulled out easily.

It took only seconds to change identity discs. Back I crept, dragging the arm with me, to throw it into my old shellhole — the arm that belonged to the naked, faceless body there, the arm that now bore the identity disc of Joe Dexter.

I had no plan, just an exultation at cheating the future and an urge to get as far away from this spot as possible. I had no fear, either. I didn't know whose name I'd taken — all I could think of was that a body would be found and identified as Joe Dexter. And I'd be free.

So I crawled away. And the Helli came again, like a big fat bumble-bee, swooping low as I froze to the ground. Then it was gone, mumbling in the distance.

But it came back, from behind this time, and, the smell of death in my nostrils, I ran.

There was a building ahead of me — solid, with a large door that seemed to leap at me with every stride I took, and the drone behind me was rising to an angry crescendo. I reached the door. There was no handle, and in a frenzy of fear I beat at it with my fists. The earth shook with a roar and the coarse grain of the door turned into heavy folds, a velvet curtain, falling over my eyes, into my nostrils and throat, choking, smothering.

And when I woke again, they told me I was William Simmons.

So that maimed and gibbering thing, who I now know to have

been Simmons, didn't die after all. He, too, had been taken to hospital, and from his identity disc they had obtained my name — Joe Dexter.

And she was there, with her scrapbook and pictures of me, from which they made him a new face — my face.

I can imagine him there, lying in his bed, his poor brain twisting in confusion, gradually coming to the conclusion that the real Joe Dexter must be dead. Listening to her reading from the scrapbook, saying nothing, but taking in everything about my past — convincing himself that he could carry on the bluff.

It must have been a bad moment for him, though, when I told him my name was William Simmons. I remember his expression. It seemed strange to me then — fearful and doubtful at the same time — but as the conversation progressed, other emotions were reflected in his features. I understand them now — hope, the saving thought that Simmons was a common enough name and in this case merely a coincidence, and finally conviction and complete relief.

God, that's ironic. It was the feeling of relief that loosened his tongue — and because he talked so freely, I killed him. And there's an ultimate irony, too. They're going to hang me tomorrow for killing Joe Dexter. They're going to execute me for murdering myself. But surely, if it wasn't Dexter who was my victim — No, that's no use. I killed a man, whatever he called himself.

A cowardly crime, the judge said. Good. Then I'll go to the scaffold as William Simmons, the coward — and Simmons *was* a coward. And Joe Dexter will have died a brave man — appropriate, too, because he always was a brave man.

Cowardice? Bravery? How much do they really depend on the outward show of things? If she could have seen him cowering in the shellhole, heard his whimpering fear, could she ever have brought herself to marry such a man? Even when his soul became obvious to her, she made allowances because she thought he was Joe Dexter.

Yet she talked to me, poured out her heart, though she thought I was a coward and she hated cowardice. I wonder why. Perhaps she recognised something about me even behind the scar. Maybe with some dim, imperceptible sense her spirit saw in me the essence of the man she really loved.

No, why should I bluff myself now? Fundamentally, I'm a coward, too — what happened on the battlefield proves that. Not like Simmons — not afraid of death, but of life. In my own way as great a craven.

There's something in *The Merchant of Venice* — how does it go?

> *"How many cowards, whose hearts are all as false*
> *As stairs of sand, wear yet upon their chins*
> *The beards of Hercules and frowning Mars,*
> *Who, inward searched, have livers white as milk,*
> *And these assume but valour's excrement*
> *To render them redoubted."*

"Did you call, Simmons?"
   "Oh — sorry, warder. No, just another habit. Reciting aloud."

LIFE SENTENCE

Tony Wilmot

Snuggling up to her husband in the early-morning warmth of the double bed, Pamela said hopefully: "Tom, I've been thinking. . . ."

"The answer's no," he snapped.

"How can you say that, Tom? You don't even know what. . . ."

"Adoption is out," he cut in. "O-u-t."

"But I'm sure we'd qualify," she persisted. "We're the right age and you're earning good money." He was already out of bed and on his way to the bathroom door.

"Will you look at the time, for God's sake! How could you let me oversleep, today of all days? I'm warning you. If I don't make TR's meeting on time, I'm holding you personally responsible." The bathroom door slammed behind him.

Sometimes Pamela found it hard to believe she had once loved Tom to distraction. Looking at herself in the mirror, now, eyes half-closed with sleep, hair uncombed, lines etched around her mouth, she felt a smouldering, almost murderous fury toward him. How had she let herself get into this situation? Why hadn't she had the guts to stand up to Tom? Guts to say, No, dammit, I won't let you assume the right to make the decisions. But Tom *had* decided; and she had allowed him to ride roughshod over her objections. Tom never consulted her about household affairs, never sought her opinion, never asked if she was happy . . . she might just as well be invisible.

Pamela parted the curtains. Clear sky. Another hot day. Thank goodness it was summer. She had thought she'd go mad during that long winter. By midday it would be in the nineties . . . yet, somehow, she half expected to see snow and ice.

She could still visualise the garden as it had been a few months earlier — icicles hanging from the roofs and telephone wires, everywhere a white blanket of snow, sometimes piled up as high as three feet against the door.

Pamela hauled herself into her dressing-gown. Was this what her life had become? A robot who did the housework, cooked the meals, did the washing and ironing, provided Tom's physical needs?

No point telling Tom how much she hated living here; he would simply accuse her of finding fault because she wouldn't adapt to a new country.

He ignored the fact that she had been against emigrating from the beginning. She'd wanted to make a fresh start at home. London, maybe. Or the West Country. Why had he insisted on a place three thousand miles from everywhere and everyone she held dear?

In the living-room the TV was blaring away, exactly the way Tom liked it of a morning: news breaks, weather reports, traffic conditions. . . .

She fixed Tom's breakfast, then started ironing his blue striped shirt. No, she should never have let Tom talk her into leaving Britain. Surely they could have made a fresh start there instead of coming here? Oh, yes, Tom claimed it was for her own good. Give her a better chance of getting over Jamie's death. Fat chance! Show her a woman who could "get over" her son being killed. Tom came clattering down the stairs and started wolfing down the scrambled eggs. How are the autoroutes, Pammie? (Why did he have to call them "autoroutes" for God's sake? And Pammie! Was it too much trouble to call her Pamela?) Had they said what the traffic was like at the interchange? And would the weather be OK for golf tomorrow?

She shrugged. He didn't really expect an answer; he was merely thinking aloud. He'd only taken up golf because he'd heard that was where you made the right connections. The same reason he'd joined the ski club, country club, and camera club.

"I just hope that car's fuel-injection isn't fouled up again," he said between mouthfuls. (He eats like a conveyor belt, she thought. Hyperventilating all the time. No wonder he's complaining of stomach pains.)

"It's the big one today. The real McCoy. Every sales rep in the company will be there, trying to catch TR's eye. No way can I be late for this dialogue." He paused, anger contorting his features, making him look younger than his forty-one years. "Are you listening? I'm in the fast lane, you know. Being late isn't part of my scenario. This isn't little old take-it-easy Britain, you know. Here, every second counts if you're to get another step up the executive ladder. Did I tell you that creep Payton has got a key to the executive loo? An idiot like that."

"What does it matter, Tom?" It was old ground; they'd been over it a dozen times. "Are you sick or something? Don't you want me to get promoted? Don't you want a new Volvo instead of that heap of scrap we run?"

No, she didn't, but it was no use telling him that. "Why do you have to keep pushing yourself to the limit, Tom?"

"Do you want us to be social lepers for ever?" he bawled.

Pamela counted to five. "We can manage, Tom. You don't need to — "

"I didn't come to this country just to manage. We managed back home. We came here to get a bigger slice of the cake, remember?" You did, she thought. I came because I'm your wife.

"Another thing," he added. "I don't want to hear any more about you and those nuns. I mean, going on retreat . . . what kind of fool thing is that? Your place is here — in the home." The door slammed behind him.

From the living-room window Pamela saw him heaving up the garage door as though his life depended on it. He's heading for another of those funny turns, she thought. The last one had been three years back, but she hadn't forgotten the fright it had given them both.

Across the way Mrs Baxter was getting her kids off to school. An unreasonable envy made Pamela turn away. Jamie would have been of school age now . . . if Tom hadn't killed him. And Tom had killed Jamie just as surely as if he'd taken a gun to him in her womb.

Everyone back home had believed Tom's explanation that she had tripped and fallen down the stairs when she had been twenty weeks pregnant. Because she had loved Tom — then — she hadn't said anything different. But Tom had never wanted Jamie in the first place. He'd accused her of not taking her morning-after pill to deliberately get herself pregnant (she had taken it, but it hadn't worked).

Tom had wanted her to have an abortion. She had refused. An uneasy truce had developed. One night Tom came home drunk, spoiling for a row . . . Later, Tom swore he hadn't pushed her, but she'd known he was lying. She had been at the foot of the stairs when she came to — and she certainly hadn't fallen. The gynaecologist had done all he could ("I'm sorry, Mrs Campbell, but infertility sometimes happens after a miscarriage . . . but you mustn't give up hope of conceiving again. Miracles can happen.") But the miracle hadn't happened. And now Pamela had resigned herself to being childless.

Outside, she heard the car door slam. Then the front door banged open. Tom came stomping in, red with angry frustration.

"That damned car. Would you believe it won't start?" He seized the phone and began to dial. "The garage swore they'd fixed it. I'll sue them, see if I don't. Jesus, look at the time! Here" — he thrust the receiver at her — "tell the office I may be delayed. But I'll make it, tell them. I'll make it."

He stomped out. Pamela heard the car's starter whirring.

Tom's office came on the line and Pamela relayed his message. No, Tom was fine. Spot of car trouble. "Oh, he's just got it going," she added, seeing Tom hunched over the wheel as he nosed into the road.

As Pamela ate toast and marmalade she began to think of Jamie again. The psychiatrist at the hospital had done his best to help her cope, but she couldn't get Jamie's memory out of her mind. Jamie had been her name for him: Tom had refused to discuss the choice of name, male or female. He didn't want either.

A couple of times she had raised the question of adoption; but he'd refused to discuss that, either. They couldn't afford a family, he'd say. Why, they hadn't even got a decent car, let alone a nice house. Those things counted in this country: it wasn't like Britain where traditional values still applied. Here, they judged you on appearances, on what you'd got — and he'd still got a lot of getting to do, so she'd better forget having kids.

At 10.30 she saw Mrs Baxter's car draw up outside. On Thursday Mrs Baxter gave Pamela a lift to the hospital where she did what Tom called "Pammie's do-gooder work".

"Hi, Pam," she greeted Pamela at the door. "All set? I'm running behind schedule. I'm supposed to be meeting Dick for lunch. But I've got a dozen things to do first."

Pamela collected her things, locked up, got in the car. As they drove the talk somehow got round to Tom. His obsession about bettering himself was getting her down, Pamela confided. "When you and Dick came over to dinner the other night, didn't you notice he talked of nothing else?"

"I guess so," Joan Baxter said. "But Dick did his fair share. That's men for you."

"I'm serious, Joan. Business, business, he thinks of nothing else. Sometimes I think I'll go out of my mind."

"He'll calm down, Pam. Just give him time."

At the hospital's social welfare office there was minor panic. Two volunteer workers hadn't turned up, so could Pamela take over Ward B? Sure. No problem. B Ward was post-operative. Pamela went round with the mobile library and collected patients' mail.

She was kept busy until 5 pm when Tom arrived to pick her up. He was pale and more than usually tense and impatient.

As she walked out of the main entrance Pamela waved goodbye to Sister Mary. "Goodbye, Sister Mary. See you next week."

Tom's mouth tightened. Once out of earshot, he said, "Have you been talking to her again — after all I've said?"

"Of course not. Aren't I allowed to wave to someone?"

Was she sure that was all she was doing? He hadn't forgotten that crazy idea she had had about going on retreat. Had she taken leave of her senses? "Over my dead body," he'd shouted at the time. What would his boss think? "Can't ask you and your wife over to dinner, sir, the wife's in a nunnery." Why, he'd be a laughing stock.

That had been three months back. Pamela hadn't forgotten her talk with Sister Mary: she had simply stopped talking about it to Tom. She knew she would never be able to make him understand that she still needed to come to terms with Jamie's death.

"Don't you wanna hear how the sales conference went?"

No, she didn't. She'd heard it all before.

"I don't know why I bother," he said. "Why can't you take an interest in my career — like Joan does in Dick's?"

"Is that why you were playing footsie under the table with her the other night?"

"Don't talk rubbish."

He was staring at the road ahead, his knuckles showing white as he tightened his grip on the wheel.

Suddenly he braked, stopping on the hard shoulder. "Are you suggesting I'm having an affair with her?" he shouted.

"Aren't you?"

"Of course I'm damned well not. Are you nuts or something?"

He's lying, she thought. All the signs were there. Once it would have hurt her deeply. Now she felt nothing. She had had her suspicions about Joan for some time. Now Tom had confirmed it; not in so many words, of course, but she knew him better than he knew himself.

"I swear there's nothing between Joan Baxter and me," he went on. "So let's have an end to it. OK?"

"OK." He may not be having an affair with Joan Baxter, she thought; but he's certainly having an affair with someone. His pallor was more pronounced now. He was holding his head. Didn't she care that he wasn't feeling well, he whined. All this arguing wasn't helping. She'd better drive: he didn't feel up to it any more.

Pamela got into the driving seat. "Is it another of those turns?"

"Started during the conference," he said heavily. "Thought I was going to collapse . . . told them I had a migraine . . . knew they thought I was covering up because I wasn't up to the job. . . ."

"Didn't you explain, Tom?"

"You kidding? And have those back-stabbers put the boot in? More than my job's worth. They're just looking for an excuse. . . ."

Pamela wanted to drive to the doctor's surgery, but Tom wouldn't hear of it. He'd go home to bed; be all right once he'd had a rest.

And, yes, he knew the special medication he'd had prescribed back home had arrested the condition . . . but, no, he wouldn't consult a doctor here . . . once a thing like that got out, the office would fire him for sure . . . so Pamela was to say no more about it.

Tom managed to walk indoors, holding on to her arm, and slumped into a chair.

Pamela made him tea, but he couldn't drink it. He had lost the power of speech and his breathing was shallow and fluttery. Minutes later his eyes had glazed over and his skin turned waxen. For a while she stood in the middle of the room, unable to think clearly. It was an attack like he'd had back home. But the symptoms had come on far more rapidly.

Tom's eyelids had closed now. Still she couldn't bring herself to take action. Reason told her to phone for help. But a curious sensation in the pit of her stomach was rooting her to the spot.

Her eyes flew to the clock. 5.56pm. They had been home about fifteen minutes, twenty at most. She need do nothing for another fifteen minutes.

Pamela felt herself relaxing. Now that she had made the decision — what to do about Tom — she felt elated, as though a great weight had been lifted from her.

Pouring herself another cup of tea, she sat opposite Tom and thought it through. It would be going against his wishes, of course, but he was hardly in a position to object, was he? For once in her life she would be doing something she wanted to do. Her decision, not Tom's. Her responsibility, not his.

Tom's hands were very cold now. Pamela couldn't detect a pulse. There was no more time. She dialled the hospital. "Hello, emergency? My husband's had a stroke. I think he's dead. Would you get Dr Breen immediately — tell him it's an emergency . . . Name? Oh, yes . . . it's Campbell . . . yes, 49 Jefferson Avenue . . . hurry, please. I'll hold."

There, she had done it. Now it was out of her hands. The rest was up to the doctors.

Seconds later a man's voice came on the line. "Dr Breen," he said.

Pamela took a breath, then: "Can you get your team here right away — my husband's had a stroke — "

It seemed hours, but it couldn't have been more than fifteen minutes before the ambulance arrived. There was nothing for Pamela to do. She watched Dr Breen carry out his examination, heard him pronounce Tom dead, then put her signature to the forms he handed her.

Pamela, sitting opposite the grey-haired woman, decided the interview had gone better than she had expected. The woman's benign expression and compassionate eyes had made it so much easier to express her innermost thoughts. "This will," the older woman said slowly, "have to be a firm commitment."

Pamela nodded. She realised that. For days — in fact, ever since her husband had died — she had been thinking it over. And, yes, she had had her doubts. But now her mind was made up. There would be no turning back now.

As the older woman went on in a quiet, restful voice, Pamela reflected on the TV news the week before. A strange shiver had run up her spine as she had listened to the newscaster's announcement: "Three patients at the City Hospital are today enjoying a new lease of life as the result of transplant operations — cornea graft, heart transplant and a kidney transplant. All three recipients are said to be 'doing fine'. The hospital's senior surgeon says that the remarkable thing about the operations is that the cornea and organs were all taken from the body of one donor. . . ."

To Pamela, it had seemed right that Tom, having taken Jamie's life, should provide the means of giving life to others. That was why, now, she felt little sense of guilt for not having told the doctors about Tom's weird affliction. Catatonic coma was how the doctors back home had described it — a rare condition in which bodily functions were reduced to the absolute minimum, enough to sustain life but mimicking death.

"You do realise," the benign woman added, "that we are an enclosed order here . . . that once admitted you will renounce all worldly possessions and cease to have contact with the outside world?"

"I'm looking forward to it," Pamela said.

THE MADONNA OF THE FOUR-ALE BAR

Basil Copper

1

Medwin felt depressed. The flat, grey streets of South London in the November rain had never looked so bleak and hopeless. The bus lurched and slithered as it turned a corner, the noses of the passengers pressed against the bleared panes, the smell of damp upholstery like decay in his nostrils. The slate roofs of the houses slid past like so many tombstones under the dark sky.

A dazzle of neon from an Odeon; a flare of sudden light from a fish-and-chip shop; the rubble of a bomb-site like a rotting tooth; and then the newsagent's shop, which was where he got off. He stood abruptly, a tall, rather absent-minded-looking man in an anonymous belted raincoat, his face dark and sardonic under the trilby hat.

He was turned forty now and knew that he would never be the success he had once hoped; the war had been over for more than a year and the supervisory job he had been promised had passed to a younger man. The stale smell of defeat hung about him. He was still what he had been in the Twenties, an unsuccessful salesman with a beat that took in all the seedy and unprofitable areas of the capital.

He had never married, though he had had his chances; the time was passing, and his cheap lodgings near Lewisham, together with his meagre salary and shabby clothing, were hardly calculated to impress a prospective fiancée. He bared his teeth in a somewhat wolfish smile, prompting the conductress who hovered at the bottom of the staircase to embark on some feeble witticism.

It was lost on Medwin. He never even heard the comment.

Only the thin, shrill punctuation of the bell as she urged the bus on, seemed to burn into his nerves like acid. He hesitated on the pavement, oblivious of the passing crowds. It was almost dusk and the rain was still falling, dropping relentlessly on his hopeless face. He had two more calls to make before he went home. The word was a mockery under the circumstances, but he persisted in using it.

He crossed the pavement quickly, spurred into action by the coldness and persistence of the rain, which was penetrating the collar of his raincoat and finding its way down on to the shoulders of his cheap suit. He opened the door of the shop and eased into its warm and garish interior. He rested his sample case on the counter and waited patiently in the queue until it was his turn to be served.

The headline of the evening paper, bundled near him, caught his eye. He smiled nervously. There had been another murder, it appeared. That made the fifth since the winter had begun. It was a woman this time. Three men and two women so far. He smiled again, aware that the fat woman behind the counter had an anxious eye on him. Impulsively, for no reason at all, he picked up the newspaper.

He would read it over his tea. Later he would cut out the article for his collection. He glanced hastily at the main details of the story. This one was near Catford; a girl of twenty-five. Like all the others, she had been strangled. THE NOOSE MURDERS, the newspaper had headlined it. He became aware of the man in front of him. He was talking to the woman who owned the shop.

"He seems to prefer this district. Lewisham, two in Forest Hill, now Catford."

The woman nodded soberly.

"He must be a madman. It all seems absolutely purposeless."

The man in front of him agreed, and after a moment or two they passed on to other topics as he completed his purchases. Medwin had moved up to the counter, the newspaper held irresolutely in his hand. He bought a packet of Park Drive as well as the paper. A short while later he was outside the shop. He paused on the pavement, aware of the sharp sting of the rain on his face. The door had opened behind him. The fat woman stood there, her cardigan blowing in the wind, one hand on his shoulder.

"You forgot your case."

Medwin turned, stammering.

"Thank you very much."

The woman looked at him strangely, as though she could read his history.

"Are you ill? You don't look well to me."

He shook his head, turning away from her friendly concern; suddenly impatient and savage. Why wouldn't people leave him alone? His headache was back. The case felt heavy in his hand; his job, his circumstances, his whole life hopeless. He turned up a side street, his last two calls forgotten. He must get in somewhere; somewhere where there was a little comfort, a little warmth. A place where he could become anonymous among a mass of people.

He crossed the road, the traffic an unheeded blur, slipping through gaps with the skill of long practice. He reached the opposite pavement, found the entrance to a small court which seemed a quiet haven after the roar of the High Street. He walked down, his footsteps echoing loudly in the confined space. The street lamps were lit and his shadow, thin and elongated, marched jerkily with him.

There was a public house in the far corner. Lights shone from it and the hubbub of voices reached his ear even from that distance. Its name composed itself before him in the watery dusk as he walked quickly towards it. The Marquis of Granby. It looked all right. He hesitated at the brassy entrance porch, his tiredness suddenly dropping from him. Medwin pushed the glass door, the newspaper still in his hand. Raucous laughter and the babble of many voices greeted him as he went in.

2

He ordered a brown ale and sat down with it in the far corner. The big, shabby room was filled with people, the air thick and stale with tobacco and cigar smoke. The latter emanated from the publican, a large, red-faced man with greasy black hair, who moved about the bar and mingled with the customers in a familiar, back-slapping manner. As he sipped at his drink Medwin studied the newspaper. The reports had a fascination for him. The facts were few; The South London Horror, as the garish sub-heading put it, was confined to a half dozen staccato paragraphs.

The girl had been strangled in cheap lodgings in a terrace house off the Catford High Road the previous night. No one had seen the man leave or enter. The ligature had been pulled so tight round the girl's neck that it had buried itself deep in the throat. Just like all the others. And, just like all the others, the instrument of death had been removed.

"An early arrest is expected," said a coarse-looking man at a table near Medwin.

He had glanced over and seen the cause of the salesman's absorption. The unwanted acquaintance winked broadly.

"We all know what that means."

Medwin nodded without speaking. He picked up his glass and half-turned in his seat, blocking out the intruder. He looked nervously at his sample case down near his feet. It would not do to forget that here. It would not be returned as it had been by the woman who ran the newsagency. He let the fragmented conversation in the bar wash over him.

There was a gas fire near his seat, giving off an agreeable heat, and steam was rising from his sodden raincoat. He began to be permeated by a sense of well-being. He turned back to the newspaper, aware that the coarse-looking man still had a liquor-bright eye on him.

There was a blurred photograph of the girl; the picture was so bad and the reproduction so imperfect in the printing that the features were unrecognisable.

A burst of laughter came from close by. It was so sudden that it startled Medwin. He looked up, vaguely aware that it seemed to emanate from the Four-Ale Bar, which was separated from the big main bar by a serving hatch. Another gust of laughter came through and Medwin could hear a girl's voice. It was a young voice, full of confidence and laughter. The jokes must have been good ones because a third explosion of mirth followed almost immediately. A group of people moved away from the bar and Medwin was able to see through into the four-ale.

She was a good-looking girl; about twenty-five to thirty, with long blonde hair. When she opened her wide, generous mouth to laugh she revealed teeth like seed-pearls.

The man with the nudging voice at the other table broke in again.

"That's Sandra. Everyone around here knows her."

Medwin shot him a quick glance in which dislike quickened to resentment at the coarse man's proprietorial air. Before Medwin could answer, the other, taking his silence for implied approval, went on quickly.

"We call her the Madonna of the Four-Ale Bar."

He licked a bluish tongue round shining lips in a manner which Medwin found extremely unpleasant.

"All right, eh?" the coarse man went on.

He paused significantly.

"If you like that sort of thing."

Medwin gave him a non-committal glance. He did not wish to offend, but the other's voice and manner was beginning to grate on his nerves. He wished he would finish his drink and go but an interest in the girl, Sandra, made him sit on, eyeing the other, hoping that he would volunteer further information.

It came without any prompting, as though from a tap.

"Don't be misled by her innocent looks. She's hot stuff from what I hear."

Medwin forced himself to smile.

"Likes the boys, does she?"

"Does she?"

The other moved nearer, leaning across the table.

"Older men, mostly. Not to say she isn't particular."

He paused again, fixing Medwin with a too-bright eye.

"Fancy your chances?"

Despite himself the salesman felt a flush rising to his cheeks.

"Hardly," he said. "I no longer have ambitions in that direction. But I like to see a well turned out woman. She's very well turned out."

The other put his glass down on the table with a faint clinking noise.

"Smart as paint. She's not short of money."

He was openly grinning now.

"You ought to try the four-ale some evening. She's always in there. Fond of salesmen from what I hear."

His eyes were fixed significantly on Medwin's case. Awkwardly, he pushed it to one side with his feet. He finished the ale and stood, turning up the collar of his raincoat.

"Perhaps I will," he forced himself to say.

He went out, the case heavy on his hand, keeping his head low, retaining the impression of warmth, the noise, the comforting clink of glasses and the animal sound of the girl's laughter through the perfect teeth.

3

It was still raining. Medwin paused in the shelter of the shop doorway, shifting the weight of the case from his left hand to his right. He had been having a tea break and the too hot liquid and the half-stale bun came back sour and treacherous in his throat. He looked up at the leaden sky; there was no lifting of the greyness and he would have to keep on at least another two hours if he was to maintain his schedule.

Kemp had been sarcastic the previous Friday at the paucity of orders. He could not afford to make an enemy of him. Jobs were hard to get with so many returning servicemen, and he had no savings to speak of. He moved off down the street, keeping in the shelter of the buildings, his mind preoccupied with the brief image of the girl's face the previous night. He wondered whether she would be there again this evening.

He had thought about her as he lay on his bed in front of the gas fire in his cheap rented room. He had the light off and in the shimmering flicker of the fire he seemed to see the muscles of her throat and the glint of the even white teeth as she gave vent to that brassy laugh. What had that man called her? Sandra. That was it. Hot stuff, he had said in his cheap, knowing way. Medwin felt the waves of warmth break across him again; half pleasure, half nausea. He had only seen the upper portion of the girl's body. He wondered what the rest of her figure would have been like. What she would be like unclothed?

He changed direction aimlessly, aware once again of the raw November air, the dingy street, the rain driving into his face, finding every interstice in his cheap clothing. He was opposite a newspaper seller's kiosk now; his eye was taken by the fluttering banner of the yellow paper placard. Heavy black type that screamed at the passers-by. SIXTH NOOSE MURDER. South London Horror.

Medwin paused. A printed poster; that meant the story would have been in the morning edition. The late ones usually had the newspaper seller's hand-pencilled scrawl. He had missed the paper that morning when he went out; he usually glanced at the one his landlady had delivered. Normally it was lying in the hall when he left, but this morning she must have picked it up earlier for it was not on the mat when he quitted the house.

He bought another newspaper now, glanced at the headlines, which repeated the legend on the placard, and folded it, thrusting it into his raincoat pocket. He made the rest of his calls perfunctorily, thinking only of the heading on the placard and the face of the blonde girl in the Four-Ale Bar. He had a lot of walking to do and was thoroughly wet and chilled when he finished for the day.

It was already a quarter past six when he caught the bus. He alighted in front of the newsagent's shop and bought his usual packet of Park Drive. The ten cigarettes had to last him the evening and all of the following day. He crossed the road and found the courtyard. At the far end the lights of the Marquis of Granby glowed invitingly.

But a disappointment awaited him. When he looked through the hatch the Four-Ale Bar was empty. Medwin bit back his sense of anti-climax. He ordered a brown ale and carried it to the corner he had occupied before. There were not so many people in this evening; perhaps it was because it was mid-week and pay packets became a little harder to stretch as the days progressed to Friday.

Fortunately, there was no sign of the odious man of the previous night and Medwin sat back, enjoying the warmth of the gas fire and the beer. He pulled the newspaper from his pocket and dried it at the fire. Then he began to read the lead story on the front page.

It was a very familiar one to him. It was a man on this occasion, the venue another cheap lodging near Lewisham. A noose had again been used, the murderer had escaped unseen. The motive was apparently robbery, as in most of the reported cases. The story had been padded out in the usual journalistic fashion, the sparse facts of last night's killing expanded with details of the earlier crimes, police interviews of outstanding banality and a list of the previous victims.

Medwin's attention soon drifted away. He could not concentrate and found first his mind and then his eyes wandering. Ever and again they came back to the hatch on the far side of the counter which gave on to the Four-Ale Bar. The trouble was the headaches; they had been getting worse lately. Medwin had difficulty sometimes in even remembering events which had occurred only a few hours previously.

It was becoming a worry in his job; on a number of occasions the customers had noted it and once he had forgotten a substantial order completely, until the client phoned Kemp. Now he put everything down in a small notebook just as soon as the order was given. He kept the notebook next to his wallet, which usually contained the money he had taken for the orders. He paid it in at the end of the week.

The wallet was getting unusually bulky with today's successes; perhaps he ought to take it in to the office tomorrow. He usually left it to the end of the week but lately things had been so bad that even the total amount had been derisive. But today had been different somehow. Perhaps things were taking a turn for the better. He got up, ordered another brown ale from the red-faced landlord and resumed his seat.

There were a number of people at the other end of the bar but it was very quiet compared to the previous evening. Medwin tried to think back. Strangely, everything that had happened after his sight of the girl had gone from his mind. He remembered only walking out of the public house and making for his lodgings. He supposed he must have sat on his bed for a while and perhaps dozed by the gas fire, but the whole of the evening had been a blur. His clothes had been wet and muddy when he awoke this morning but that was nothing unusual. He had had several blank spots in his memory the past few months. Perhaps he ought to consult a doctor.

Medwin surreptitiously glanced at his cheap Swiss wristwatch. He had bought it in Gibraltar during the war but despite its dubious origin it kept remarkably good time. Already he had been here an hour. He looked up suddenly. The door to the Four-Ale Bar had opened; the landlord strode swiftly to the hatchway and there was the same brassy laugh, ringing out through the unaccustomed hush of the Marquis of Granby.

Without knowing what he was doing, Medwin was round and into the other section, his sample case banging heedlessly against the partition. The girl was exceptionally good-looking. She glanced at him gravely, pushing one strand of her long blonde hair back from her eyes as he came up.

"Good evening, miss. Care for a drink?"

Medwin's voice was hurried, uncertain, as he blurted out his crude invitation. The girl smiled, showing him the teeth like seed-pearls.

"I don't mind. A gin and tonic please, Cecil."

The landlord gave Medwin a knowing look and went back along the bar. Medwin put down his case and hat, the newspaper fluttering to the floor. The girl stooped to pick it up for him and their heads almost touched. Medwin laughed nervously, the girl full-throatedly. She fumbled in her bag, produced a cigarette. Medwin lit it for her with his silver lighter, bought in a fit of extravagance before the war; perhaps the only decent thing he owned. Fortunately it lit first time. The girl's eyes widened as she blew smoke out.

"I don't think I've seen you here before, Mr. . . . ."

"Medwin. Call me George."

The pale blue eyes raked over him insolently.

"All right, George. My name's Sandra. Shall we sit in the corner? It's more comfortable there."

The girl preceded him into the small cubicle and Medwin was able to admire the slim, straight suppleness of her figure. He hurriedly put down his hat, sample case and newspaper and went back for the drinks. When he returned the girl was sitting with her legs crossed, showing a generous expanse of silken thigh. She was studying the newspaper and did not look up until he put down the drink.

"Cheers."

She drank slowly, fastidiously, as though her glass held nectar; she reminded Medwin of nothing so much as an exotic bird drinking at some tropical stream. She smiled again as she noticed him studying her. Medwin cleared his throat diffidently.

"You seem to be very popular, Sandra."

He lingered over the last word, savouring it on his tongue for the first time. The girl's eyes held his own for a fraction longer than was necessary.

"Oh, you mean last night? Were you here last night?"

Medwin nodded, cautiously tasting his drink.

"We had a good crowd in last night. The Granby's very crowded on certain evenings of the week. I don't remember seeing you before."

Medwin shook his head.

"I only found it by accident."

The pink tongue explored the full lower lip and the flash of white teeth was enticingly close.

"I hope you'll come again. I have to go soon."

Medwin's stab of disappointment was ridiculously poignant. After all, he had only known the girl a few minutes. But he masked his feelings and stared down into the bottom of his glass.

"Will you be here tomorrow night?"

"Yes, all the evening. From about half-past six."

"Good. I'll be here, then."

The girl was already standing up, draining her drink quickly. Her eyes were fixed somewhere over Medwin's shoulder as he rose awkwardly too. Medwin glimpsed a tall, burly man in a houndstooth sports jacket through the frosted glass of the window. To Medwin's surprise the girl held out her hand to him in a formal gesture. Her skin was warm and soft to the touch.

"Until tomorrow, then. Thanks for the drink."

Her high heels rat-tatted over the linoleum of the Four-Ale Bar and then she was gone, with a wave to the landlord. A few moments later the roar of a powerful sports car echoed down the court. Medwin sat down with a distinct sense of anti-climax. His headache was back again. He finished his brown ale, ordered another and sat on as though in a daze. It was quite late by the time he left the bar.

4

A week had gone by. Medwin had seen the girl three times. Once alone and on two other occasions surrounded by a large group of youngish men. She seemed to have an inexhaustible supply of male acquaintances of a rather raffish and seedy type, and on those evenings Medwin had sat shyly on the fringe of the crowd, speaking only when he was spoken to. But he bought his rounds with the rest of them and seemed to have won a grudging acceptance as the week passed.

Medwin's own fortunes had taken a slight upward turn. Kemp had hinted that there might be a supervisory position going in the next few months. He would have twelve salesmen working under him and would take a percentage of their commission. Medwin became conscious of the rough surface of his sample case on the bus seat beside him as he rested his hand on it. He strained to see through the bleared panes but he was still three stops off yet.

The girl seemed to have brought him luck. The last week had been a good one and his wallet held more than fifty pounds in small denomination notes and he had a number of promises for large orders the following week. He had finished early tonight; he wanted to be in good time. He and Sandra would have a drink at the pub and later she had agreed to go back to his lodgings for some supper. Medwin's landlady was away at the moment and as her lodgers all had their own keys to the street door there would be no awkward questions asked about his lady visitor.

It was still day and the crimson disc of the sun stained the whole horizon so that the curtain of falling rain and the shimmer on the roof tops looked wine-red in the fading light. He got off at the newsagent's and sprinted across the pavement to the doors. He saw the placard long before he got there. Yet another one; a woman again, apparently.

He bought an evening paper with his packet of Park Drive and decided to save it until he reached the pub. He ate a snack at a small café in the next street, waiting until darkness. Sandra would not be on time. He had noticed she was invariably half an hour later than the time appointed, so he did not hurry as he directed his steps toward the quiet court with its old-fashioned street lamps. He was quite wet by the time he reached the doors; the Four-Ale Bar was empty, as he had expected, and he took off his raincoat and sat near the fire while he waited for his order.

If it were not for the headaches he would be quite contented; there was a heavy weight across his forehead at the moment which seemed to clamp his skull in a crushing grip. He closed his eyes to ease the pain and when he opened them saw the landlord staring at him anxiously from the bar.

"Are you all right? You went quite white just then."

Medwin got up and went toward him. The pain was receding now.

"Just tired. It was a rough day today."

Cecil nodded sympathetically.

"The weather doesn't help."

He moved away as a customer called from the lounge bar and Medwin resumed his seat, aware of perspiration on his forehead and a pulse hammering in his throat. He caught sight of himself in one of the cracked mirrors in the Victorian gilt mounting. He looked quite presentable except for a whiteness around the eyes and mouth. He lifted his glass, letting the thick, sluggish liquid ease its way slowly down his throat.

Then he looked at the paper. The big black heading shouted: SOUTH LONDON HORROR, NOOSE MURDERER STRIKES AGAIN. Beneath the banal emotion and the cheap writing Medwin sensed the squalor and the sordidness of the crimes. He read on, his beer untasted. The name of the victim meant nothing, as always. A young girl this time, secretary in a shipping office; the weekly pay packet in her purse the pathetic motive, apparently. Medwin looked up, his headache forgotten, as he heard the click of the bar door. The girl was there, wearing a fur-trimmed coat. She looked vivid and appealing in her blonde healthiness as she tossed the long, rain-flecked hair back from her shoulders.

"Been waiting long?"

"Only a few minutes," Medwin lied.

He got up to get her a drink. He knew what she would have without being asked now. He could not resist flourishing the large wad of banknotes as he opened his wallet. The girl's eyes glistened as she caught the movement; she was obviously impressed, Medwin thought with quiet satisfaction. His luck was beginning to change at last. As he came back to the table where Sandra sat, glowing and vibrant beneath the shimmer of the bar lamps, he felt a small core of contentment growing within him; something he had not really felt since the carefree pre-war days.

When they left more than an hour later they were arm in arm. Medwin had had a little too much to drink but he was still in control of himself. He had suggested a cab but the girl had laughed, asking how they would find one in South London without ringing a hire firm. Instead they sauntered, like a couple window-shopping; it was still spitting with rain, but not unpleasantly so, and the neon signs and the lights of the shop windows were reflected in dazzling patterns from the wet pavements until the drab background of streets looked like an Impressionist painting.

Medwin smiled to himself; it was obviously the girl's presence and the drinks that were responsible for his euphoric mood. Normally he walked on his rounds conscious only of the grim blackness of his surroundings. Tonight, instead of being cheap and garish, the milieu might have been Mayfair.

They had talked of trivialities in the pub, only once touching on the subject that seemed to occupy everybody else in these areas. Medwin had produced his newspaper, tapped the headlines with his forefinger.

"Aren't you afraid to be out alone at night with that creature around?"

The girl had smiled contemptuously.

"Why should I be? People are stupid to get themselves into such situations. If they don't let him in how can they be harmed?"

Medwin was struck by the logic of her remark.

"Even so," he said, "you should choose your friends with care. You know very little about me."

They were passing an arcade ablaze with light at the time and the shadows, tinted with red, green and gold fell across the girl's face. She looked at him with wide eyes, an expression on her features he had come to know.

"I know all I care to know," she said. "You are kind and generous. There is a good deal more to you than most people notice on the surface."

That was true at any rate, Medwin thought, as he surreptitiously shifted the weight of his sample case from one hand to another. They paused on the pavement to allow a bus to pass. On the opposite side of the road the district changed. The shops were meaner, dark and shuttered. People did not waste electricity here. The orange street lamps cast a leprous light and shone in a melancholy manner on Medwin's cheekbones and eyeballs and made them glint menacingly in the amber shadows.

"Perhaps," he said jokingly. "For all you know my case may be full of the tools of my trade. My strangling rope, my gloves — and the booty taken from my victims."

The girl smiled almost dreamily. They were passing under a railway viaduct at the time, a sombre place, where seeping water made slimy patches on the brickwork. The thunder of a passing train made her answer unintelligible. Steam and smoke whirled about the gloomy cavern and red sparks danced in the wind. The lights from the passing carriages made mocking masks of their features and Medwin asked her to repeat her remark as the train receded angrily into the distance.

They were under the arch now and her voice came clear and firm, amplified by the confined surroundings.

"It's all a question of reading character and confidence, isn't it?"

Medwin nodded,

"I suppose so," he said diffidently.

Her face looked more like a madonna than ever, he thought, as she leaned toward him. She looped her arm more tightly in his and pressed against him affectionately as they came out from the archway and turned to the right at Medwin's direction. His place was only two streets away now and as the rain was again slanting down he was glad when they got in the shelter of the porch.

He did not put on the light in the communal hallway but his precaution was not needed; his landlady was indeed away and no one saw them as they ascended quietly to the third floor. This was ideal for Medwin's purposes and his heart was thumping a little as he put his key in the lock-plate of the door.

His attempts to brighten the drab room were amateurish in the extreme, but Sandra did not seem to notice. He put on the lamp with the red silk shade that stood near the divan-bed. He had left the gas fire on low, so that the room was agreeably warm. With the fire turned up, the curtains drawn against the dampness and the night, and the red-shaded lamp, the ugliness of the surroundings was forgotten.

Medwin put his sample case down near the bed and washed his hands in the basin in the far corner. They ate at a small table near the gas fire; Medwin had even purchased a bottle of white wine the evening before and the meal took on the semblance of an occasion. The girl had taken off her coat and afterwards, her chair pushed back, she smoked a cigarette in a green jade holder while her silken legs shimmered excitingly in the lamplight.

She wore a tight brown sweater which emphasised her firm breasts and her eyes looked at him mockingly as though they had already divined his intention. Medwin pushed his chair back too and cleared his throat.

"Wouldn't you be more comfortable over here?"

"If you prefer."

There was neither provocation nor lack of interest in the voice; it was bland and neutral. Medwin felt disappointed. But later, drinking the third glass of wine with Sandra warm and co-operative on the divan beside him, he had revised his opinion.

"Here, let me," she said calmly, amused at his inexpert efforts.

She turned away from him, pulled the sweater up over her head with a supple movement of her lithe brown arms. Medwin was at a loss. He found himself dry-mouthed and lacking initiative. Instinctively, he turned away, found his unseeing eyes focused on the sample case near his feet. His headache had quite gone now.

"Haven't you seen a woman before?" Sandra said.

Her voice was low and innocent. She glanced at his turned back with bright, comprehending eyes. She looked very beautiful at that moment. She seemed to understand Medwin's continued silence. Then she reached in the open mouth of her handbag. She brought out the pair of wire cheese-cutters with the wooden handles. They glinted in the lamplight as she slipped the loop swiftly over Medwin's head.

Her lips were parted voluptuously, her tongue lolling from between them in a delicious parody of Medwin's own attitude. The choking noises went on but the girl's thoughts were far away. The salesman's wallet had fallen from his jacket pocket in his involuntary struggles. The Madonna of the Four-Ale Bar increased the pressure on the handles.

Medwin had died without realising it. Even before he had stopped breathing she was reaching out for the bundle of notes.

LAST POST

Jean McConnell

Joleyn in Wisconsin hesitated, her pen poised over the note-paper. It certainly wasn't an easy letter to compose, but she had to do it.

"Dear Eddie," she wrote, then sat back anxiously. It was important that she worded it correctly. So much depended on the reply. "I'm so worried," she continued.

What has happened? The usual date has come and gone with no communication from you. This is the first time you have ever let me down. You see how I have come to rely on your good nature!

I wouldn't have written, but it is about little Teddie. In the last month I've been told there's a surgeon who has perfected an operation which could mean Teddie might be able to walk. I know you will understand what this means to the boy. And I'm sure it would make you happy to think he could run and play and have fun.

You know I have always paid up on the insurance that you took out for us; as you appreciated, medication is so expensive here. But this new operation, while it sounds like some kind of miracle, will cost far more than the policy will cover.

Teddie is thrilled, and not at all scared, but you know he's a brave kid. How could he not be with such a father? There must have been some mistake, as I'm sure you would never want us to be in this situation. You know how grateful I have always been for your attitude to things, and you know I wouldn't be writing to you now if it wasn't so very urgent and important to Teddie. As always. Joleyn.

She addressed an envelope to Colonel Grant-Poole in Dorset, England, then went down town to mail it.

Mrs Felicity Grant-Poole opened the letter a few days later. At first the contents bewildered her, then their implication gradually became clear. She let the letter fall on her lap and her eyes filled with tears.

With blurred vision she read it again. This was from a woman with a child whom Edward had been supporting. On the other side of the world were two human beings who had a claim on him. It could only be for one reason: the woman must have been Edward's mistress!

But when? Where? Felicity had never had the slightest suspicion. She thought of Edward and found herself puzzled as well as deeply hurt. She had always trusted him so implicitly — had believed him to be so completely honourable. The thought that he had hidden this secret from her for years gave her a pain so great she thought she would faint.

Felicity rose and moved across the room to look at a portrait of Edward, gazing at her with steadfast eyes, wearing his uniform with the well-earned medals. It was a painting commissioned by the men of his regiment. He had been greatly loved. The words mocked her. Greatly loved!

Felicity went to her elegant little desk and sat down to write. In the American custom there was a name and address on the envelope.

Dear Miss Eastmen,

Your letter to Colonel Grant-Poole has come into my hands. This has occurred because the Colonel died three months ago and, as his widow, all correspondence is delivered to me. You obviously have not been informed of his death. I am sorry for the necessity of writing to you with this unexpected news.

Felicity paused. What more was there for her to say? That the letter had come as a great shock to her, still grieving as she was

for the husband she had loved so deeply? No, the fact of
Edward's death was all that was called for.

She signed the letter and rang for her housekeeper, who took it
down to the village and posted it.

Felicity told no one of her news. She bore the pain by herself.
She was determined no hint of her husband's secret should get
out. She was sure it was a secret, for she knew his strength of
character in that respect at least. No one must ever know of this
aberration — so out of keeping with Edward's normal nature.

It must have occurred at some time when Edward was on tour
of duty overseas. She'd have liked to think that it was long ago,
but obviously a young child ruled that out.

Felicity could, perhaps, have put thoughts of the woman from
her mind in time, but the image of the invalid child returned to
her thoughts regularly. She herself had two healthy and beautiful
daughters and three grandchildren. She could feel compassion
for the unfortunate little boy.

Joleyn, in Wisconsin, read the letter from Felicity, and immediately replied.

Dear Mrs Grant-Poole,
      I feel I must apologise most sincerely for everything that
has happened. I was shocked by the news about Ed

— Joleyn crossed the letters out, substituted 'the Colonel', and
then went on —

I cannot tell you how sorry I am to have added to your
troubles. It was never the intention that you should be in any
way hurt by what was only a very short-lived personal
relationship between your husband and myself.
      If it hadn't been for the birth of my son, the friendship would
have ceased long ago. But when the baby came, the Colonel
was very generous to me. Then, when it was discovered that
Teddie had this crippling disease, so that I had to stay at home
and nurse him, the Colonel insisted on sending me regular

financial support. Without this I truly do not know what would have become of us.

It was understood that I'd never make contact with the Colonel in any way, and I would never have done so except that I had received no allowance this quarter, at a time when such a wonderful opportunity had arisen for my boy. I had no intention of injuring you. I wrote in desperation. I believed that if he knew the money had gone astray, he'd immediately deal with it. Now, of course, I know the true facts.

I hope you can bring yourself to forgive me for writing and also that you can put the whole matter out of your mind. I consider myself lucky to have known such a kind man as the Colonel and to have had his support. It is more than I deserved. But I know he did it for the sake of Teddie, who is just an innocent victim, of course. Believe me, I will never refer to this thing again, as the last thing I would want is for the Colonel's reputation to suffer.

Felicity sat reading Joleyn's latest letter. She had burnt the former one in fear that one of her daughters might discover it at some time in the future and be upset.

Her heart pounded painfully. She tried to envisage this woman with whom her husband had been so intimate. What did she look like? That she existed at all was still almost impossible for Felicity to accept. Edward with his gentle, caring nature, his devotion to his daughters, his loyal affection for her. Or so she had believed.

No, she mustn't think along those lines! His love for her had never changed. This liaison must have been the result of some exceptional situation. She must remember him as he had always been — a good, kind, thoughtful man of great integrity.

Because of this, Felicity knew what Edward would have wanted her to do now. Knew it as clearly as if he had been there to tell her, speaking in his deep calm voice, looking at her with his honest eyes. Yes, there was no doubt of it. The child was Edward's son. His flesh and blood. Felicity reached for her cheque book.

The cheque that arrived in Joleyn's mailbox was very generous indeed. The Colonel had left Felicity well provided for, and she had made some discreet enquiries about medical costs in the United States. She had sent the sort of amount she believed would cover the cost of the operation and treatment, with a substantial sum in addition.

Joleyn finished packing her suitcases. There was nearly an hour to wait before her taxi was due to arrive. Just in time, she thought, to draft another letter before she left to catch the plane for her month's vacation in Hawaii. It got more and more expensive there, but what the hell. Now, where had she put that copy of *The Times* her cousin had obligingly sent her from London? She glanced at her watch. Yes, she still had at least half an hour. Joleyn settled into her soft leather lounger. She ran her expensively manicured finger down the obituary column. Ah, there was a promising one. 'Robert Peregrine Walsingham, aged 57. Suddenly at The Priory, Diddingcote, Berkshire.' Joleyn picked up her pen.

"Dear Robert," she wrote, "I'm so very worried, I can't think why you haven't been in touch as normal. Little Bobby has been having a lot more of his attacks. . . ."

She'd just rough the letter out, much as usual. Time enough to send it off in a couple of months.

THE RULES OF THE GAME

George Sims

Leslie Mercer looked on life as a game and believed it was a game that he was good at, generally obeying the rules but twisting them when it suited him. He would refer to these rules in a sardonic way when he heard of another's misfortunes, for he always took other people's tragedies equably, remarking *sotto voce* "Ah, the rules of the game" when he heard that an acquaintance had lost a child or was ill with cancer.

A London orphan, Leslie Mercer had only a sketchy education and his expertise as an estate agent had come from hard-won experience. At fifteen he had started work as an office boy with one of London's most prestigious firms in Knightsbridge, but he knew that his prospects would be limited there as all the top jobs were held by men who had been to university and had degrees. After Knightsbridge, Mercer had worked with other estate agents in Hendon, Golders Green and Hampstead. The high-powered Jewish firm, Gimbel & Co., of Hampstead High Street, had sacked him after only a few weeks, David Gimbel remarking, "I'm letting you go, Mercer. You push too hard or you don't push at all." The obvious unfairness of Gimbel's criticism had rankled and would never be forgotten.

With his job in Harrow Mercer felt that he had fallen on his feet. The firm, Kimberley Ross, had only been formed in 1965 but it was a thrusting, rapidly expanding one, continually opening new offices throughout Middlesex. Mercer had played a good card in realising that one of the partners, John Ross, a fat jolly widower, was open to flattery and he laid it on with a trowel. His second good card had been in wooing Ross's daughter June, a plump woman with an unhealthy complexion and very little to say. Mercer had taken these handicaps into consideration but did not hesitate to play the ace of trumps by marrying June, philosophising on the lines that the rules of the game did not allow orphans to have everything at once. As soon as he was married Mercer felt that his job was safe for life despite the fact that Alec Kimberley continued to regard him coldly.

On his marriage Leslie Mercer and his bride moved into a small semi-detached house in Treve Avenue and then they moved again, a year later, into a larger detached house in Whitmore Road. Mercer had learnt a lesson from Gimbel's reproof and had made his house-selling technique more subtle. He had also added a few longer words to his rather limited vocabulary and dragged these in at every opportunity: "A charming though bijou residence", "From a pragmatic viewpoint", "Arguably the best house in the road", "Has somewhat idiosyncratic appeal". Mercer played yet another trump in thinking of a way of advertising the firm — with a tablet advertisement that said nothing more than 'KIMBERLEY ROSS OF HARROW'. Alec Kimberley pooh-poohed the idea, calling it 'gimmicky', but he was proved wrong. The advertisement, first inserted in the *Harrow Observer* and then in other papers in neighbouring areas, aroused a lot of interest. Mercer felt that his career had peaked the first time he saw the somewhat enigmatic wording on the side of a bus.

When John Ross died of a heart attack in the middle of a grandiloquent statement from behind his imposingly large desk, Mercer greeted the news with his usual imperturbable remark, then added, also *sotto voce*, "My cup runneth over." John Ross left his sister ten per cent of the shares in Kimberley Ross and five thousand pounds in cash. All the rest of his shares and his considerable fortune were left to June who accepted the inheritance, as so much else, phlegmatically.

By this time Mercer was in the mood to move again and the inheritance enabled them to purchase a substantial house, called 'The Laurels', in Pinner, which Mercer invariably referred to as 'the village'. By this time he had grown very tired of June's fat, pasty face, her flabby arms and quite gross legs, but he gave considerable thought to the subject of other female company as the rules of the game would not permit the loss of his present ménage. A chance encounter with a young widow, Susan Williams, in Ealing provided the ideal opportunity, for Susan was very lively and talkative but admirably discreet; she also was slim and had an excellent complexion. Mercer's business hours were, of necessity, flexible and gave him ample opportunity to visit the Ealing flat in the evenings. Mercer was also discreet in that he made Susan Williams no rash promises, but he did not envisage spending the rest of his life watching June become heavier and heavier.

Along with 'The Laurels', the Mercers had acquired Mrs Madge Thomas, who did all the housework and enabled June to lie on a couch most of the day, watching TV and eating chocolates. Madge was a rather slow worker but she was thorough, minded her own business and was subservient — and subservience goes down rather well with an employer who has spent the first fifteen years of his life in an orphanage.

There came a time when Leslie Mercer entered his bathroom without knocking on the closed door, and viewed his wife's enormous behind with considerable distaste. He apologised, retreated quickly and spent much of the day brooding on his now intolerable marriage. June had made a simple will leaving all her possessions to her husband, so that the only thing necessary to make Mercer's life perfect was her decease. Once the thought was in his mind he found it difficult to concentrate on other matters and his attitude to business became lackadaisical — so much so that he earned a sharp reproof from Alec Kimberley. Mercer left Kimberley's office feeling that his face was stiff and red, and that he was now forced, by all the rules of the game, to take steps to place himself forever beyond such criticism. With forty per cent of the shares in the firm he would be on an even footing with Kimberley and able to call him Alec. Quite simply, it had become essential that June should die, and it was merely a question of finding some foolproof method of killing her. "Keep it simple," he urged himself, and this crucial phrase remained in his mind all day. A push on the steep stairs at 'The Laurels' seemed a possibility, for it was obvious that anyone of June's bulk and weight would fall very heavily, but there was always a chance that she might survive the fall.

"Drowning in the bath" — the simple idea popped into Mercer's head as he was driving back from Harrow to Pinner. It was as if someone had said the phrase and provided the perfect answer. A simple accident that was quite feasible if June happened to slip on the soap and fall heavily. She made a habit of taking a long bath every morning from about 8.30 am, just a quarter of an hour before Leslie Mercer departed for the office. Madge Thomas always came to work at 9 am and had her own key but often had to knock on the bathroom door for any instructions since June was fond of a 'good, long soak'. Madge would be the ideal person to discover the corpse in the bath, as she was bound to add confusion to the scene in her futile efforts to save her mistress, and could be relied on to obliterate any clues; not that Mercer expected to leave any. And the elderly family doctor, James Fothergill, was another bonus, a truly excellent person to have on the scene of the crime for he had a dull, conventional mind, and was very unlikely to have any suspicions. During a long, boring evening at 'The Laurels' while his wife was glued to the TV, Mercer went over the murder scenario again and again in his mind, and found it to be foolproof.

About a week after deciding on the method of killing June, Leslie Mercer had a particularly enjoyable evening in Susan's flat and envisaged how much better his life would be when he was no longer bound to return to the marital home. He returned to 'The Laurels' determined to carry out his plan the next morning.

At 8.35 am the following day Mercer knocked on the bathroom door, in his shirt-sleeves, then entered the steam-filled room. The window was closed and due to the steam he could only see a vague shape in the full-length mirror facing him. "A tragic accident. The perfect crime," a voice seemed to say in his ear. June was in a deep bath, eating an apple and reading a magazine. She did not look up when he entered or when he said, "Sorry about this." When he added "Junie, I've been thinking," she just muttered "What?" in her usual apathetic way. "Just this," he said, bending down and seizing her thick ankles. Using all his strength, he tugged them up nearly level with his shoulders so that her head went down under the soapy water as she uttered a squawking scream so loud he was glad that 'The Laurels' was a detached house, standing well back from the road. June kicked and struggled wildly and it was difficult to hold her beefy legs, but she did not seem to think of reaching up for the sides of the bath. She threshed about like a great beast. Terror made her try to shout, so that she kept on swallowing water and choking, which again made her open her mouth. Mercer had a ring-side seat from which to watch Death at work, realised that he was uniquely placed, so to speak, and found it all quite fascinating. He even felt like giving her advice about how to survive such an ordeal, but realised that it was against the rules of the game. Within a minute June's efforts grew feebler, but she continued to open her mouth and gulp even when her arms were only splashing feebly. All in all Mercer enjoyed the experience more than most things. When her movements ceased completely and her fixed expression was ghastly and inscrutable, Mercer allowed himself to relax and sigh without letting go of her ankles.

He held her legs for another minute then let go and stepped back, glimpsing his blurred image in the mirror with a momentary shock. "Calm down, take it easy," he advised himself in a strange-sounding voice. Then he bent down and cracked June's head against the taps. When he let go again she slid down into the foamy water with the sodden magazine and the bobbing core of the apple. Mercer took the bar of soap from its dish and dropped it into the water. "Perfect," he said. "I've committed the perfect murder, and, by all the rules of the game, it is a crime which cannot be punished." He looked round the room: the floor was very wet but it was obvious that someone of June's bulk would displace a lot of water in falling back into the bath. There were some splashes on his shirt sleeves but they would dry quickly under his jacket.

Mercer glanced at his wrist-watch and saw that it was 8.45. "Just right," he said aloud. "All quite perfect," he added, gloating at the thought of how clever he had been. He spun on his heel, anxious to be on his way, slipped on the wet floor, twisted awkwardly and fell, cracking his head hard against the edge of the door.

After what seemed only a few minutes of a horrid nightmare in which he was talking gibberish and unable to make himself understood, Mercer woke to find he was lying on the marital bed. There was a violent pain in the back of his head which seemed to be too heavy to lift; nor could he move his limbs. Four faces stared down at him sympathetically: Madge Thomas, Dr Fothergill and two ambulance men.

Madge bent down further and spoke very loudly as if he was deaf. "Mr M., can you hear me Mr M.? Oh dear, you've had such a terrible shock! Do you feel any better now, Mr M.?"

Mercer wanted to make it quite clear to Madge and the other witnesses that he had fallen while struggling to get June out of the bath, and that any splashes of water on his clothes had come about then. He thought he should say something suitable about June and the fright he had experienced in finding her dead. Instead he said slowly and distinctly, "The, them, those, this, these, they. . . ."

Dr Fothergill also bent down, saying, "Now do try to be calm, old man. It's been a bad blow, but please calm yourself. We may have to move you."

Mercer felt frustrated by Fothergill's stupidity. He shouted, "Rules, rolls, rills, reefs, reach, rat. . . ."

One of the ambulance men bent down and put a restraining hand on Mercer's shoulder. "Sir, please sir! Calm down! We have to get you on the stretcher."

Mercer screamed, "Game, gate, goat, get, going, going, gone."

GOLD SWORD

Mike Ripley

"I knew your father for over forty years," said old man Potts as soon as we were a decent distance from the grave, "and only once did he do something totally surprising."

"You mean selling the family firm, I suppose?" I tried to sound polite, but I had heard this opening gambit many times before.

"That was anything but surprising," blustered Dr Crumley ungraciously. "Think of all those takeovers in the Sixties."

There had been takeovers, of course, but my father — like many others — had sold up rather than be bought up.

"No, no," said Potts irritably, "I meant when he sent back his OBE. Returned his 'gong' as he called it. Damn funny thing to do, if you ask me."

No one had, but that was unlikely to deter the venerable editor of the *Seagrave Packet*, our noble, moral, crusading, and only local newspaper.

Nor our venerable local doctor.

"Wasn't it because of the Beatles?" Dr Crumley shouted. I had forgotten the deafness in his left ear and his assumption — odd for a medical man — that the affliction was contagious. "Didn't everybody send back their gongs in protest when the Beatles got the MBE?"

"I'd be surprised if Sydney knew who the Beatles are," said Potts.

Were, I thought; but I said nothing.

"The one thing Sydney did which shocked me," Crumley pressed on, "was when he stopped brewing Gold Sword. It wasn't long before he sold the brewery, come to think of it. That was the best barley wine I've ever drunk. Before or since."

The doctor closed his eyes to help conjure up a long-lost

flavour. "In summer, we'd drink it half-and-half with mild ale. My God, if we did that today, old Potts here would call us 'Lager Louts' in that paper of his."

"I was a bitter man myself," said Potts dreamily. "I even remember the old adverts we put in the paper: 'Seton's Seaside Ales'. But you're right for once, Crumley. Sydney's Gold Sword was a cracking beer."

Potts turned on me as we reached the churchyard gate. "Haven't you ever felt cheated of your heritage, young Pip? If Sydney hadn't sold up, you'd have been — what? — the fifth generation of Setons to run the firm?"

"Wouldn't have to work for a living, like you do now, eh?" cackled Crumley.

"Seriously, Philip," Potts persisted, "don't you resent your father selling out back in the Sixties?"

The fact that he was totally unsuitable for service in any of the armed forces on the outbreak of war in 1939 greatly depressed my father. Poor eyesight from birth and a permanent limp (acquired after a clash of wills with an unruly Percheron in 1937) ruled out his chances for the commission which so many of his brewer contemporaries proudly boasted.

He had been appointed managing director of the family brewery in early 1939 when my grandfather had inherited the chairmanship from my great-grandfather, and he had been left to "get on with it". (Grandad saw the chairmanship as a chance for early retirement to indulge his passion for bird watching; a trait, happily, not genetic.)

Newly married, in his early thirties, and mentally supremely fit, he set to with a will, pulling the brewery out of the tail-end of the Depression which had even hit our sleepy South Coast home town of Seagrave. The war only served to increase his energy supply. His own experiments with pressurised metal casks were halted and he organised the "Spitfire for Seagrave" drive to collect aluminium. He recruited local women as drivers and sales representatives to replace called-up brewery workers (they had been confined to the bottling sheds in World War I). He rationed raw materials, and then beer itself, reduced his gravities as requested, and promoted draught rather than bottled beer to save on glass, rubber and petrol. He also found time to organise Seagrave's Air Raid Precautions and then the local Home Guard, and sat on dozens of committees for fund-raising or the adoption of evacuated children.

Still it was not enough.

His chance to do more — much more — came in 1942.

For the first two and a half years of the war, brewers had supplied troop canteens with beer through their local NAAFI organisation; Seton's brewery being ideally placed to supply the army's Southern Command. Yet relations were far from smooth. Local brewers resented using their meagre petrol ration to deliver to army bases when the army seemed to have petrol to burn. The twenty-four-hour-a-day army couldn't understand why brewers could not brew any quantity desired whenever needed (immediately), or why they made such a fuss about not getting their casks back. In fact, both parties seriously wondered if the other knew there was a war on.

If civilian evacuation, the drive for munitions, conscription of brewery workers and drinking customers and air-raids had not disrupted life enough, to cap it all, the Yanks were suddenly Over Here.

By mid-1942, with the influx of Allied troops, brewers faced an extra demand for at least 600,000 barrels of beer a year, and there were already acute shortages in country pubs. But unlike the First World War, beer was seen — by a very different prime minister — as a morale-booster rather than the Germans' secret weapon. Something had to be done, and the Ministry of Food called on the Brewers' Society to establish a "Beer For Troops" committee to bring order to the growing confusion.

My father, already the company's representative at the Society, was delighted to be asked to serve. He would have been mortified not to be.

Until the war finished, he spent at least three days a month in London working for the Beer For Troops committee, each problem which came before it being examined in minute detail. Where could extra coal for malting be found? How quickly could 10,000 gross screw-stoppers be produced? What was the most economical specification for badly needed casks and crates? Which British regiments preferred dark mild to light ale? Should the brewers concentrate on producing one uniform "Army Ale"? (An overwhelming "No".) How could 200 tons of Oregon hops be kept fresh on the convoy across the Atlantic? (By lining the sacks with old newspapers!)

And not only was there the NAAFI to deal with, but a new and very demanding customer in the form of the Headquarters of Services of Supply, US Army, European Theater of Operations.

For convenience, the American supply office became known as the 'Selfridge Annex', after its allocated offices between Wigmore and Oxford Streets, and my father took it upon himself to liaise directly with the commanding officer, Colonel Garrett M. Ayres, QM. They became close friends, keeping in touch after the war. My father had often told the after-dinner story of how the Americans were not given stationery to use, as paper was in short supply, and had to conduct their correspondence on the back of pre-printed forms headed "Meat and Livestock Control — Record of Inedible Offal". Either through good manners or blissful ignorance, none of the Americans ever asked what "inedible offal" was (and much of the correspondence is still on the files).

As became his custom on his Beer For Troops days in London, my father would meet Colonel Ayres for dinner. He got into the habit of telephoning the Selfridge Annex at about 5 pm and then walking from Society headquarters in Upper Belgrave Street, arriving in time for what the US Army called the 'cocktail hour'.

On one such occasion, in January 1944, he had telephoned to Ayres and was pulling on his overcoat when one of the Society secretaries informed him there was a telephone call for him.

"Mr Seton? Mr Sydney Seton?"

"Yes."

"Mr Seton, you don't know me, b-b-but I would l-l-like to talk to you. My name is Russell, and it is, as they s-s-say, a matter of national sec-sec-security."

"Well, this is..er..not usual, er . . ." My father, unconsciously copying the caller's stutter, would have blushed at himself.

"It is irregular, Mr Seton, I g-g-grant you that, but I am in — shall we say — the irregular part of the war effort. Could you spare me a few minutes at Baker Street this evening, before you meet Colonel Ayres?"

"If it's important, of course. Whereabouts?"

"The bottom end of Baker Street, at Portman Square. As soon as you can, if that's all right."

Intrigued — how had Russell known about Colonel Ayres? — my father set out, skirting Hyde Park. As the Blitz was over and the V-bombs had not yet replaced the Luftwaffe, the main hazard in the blackout was London's black, almost invisible, cabs.

Harold Russell, as he introduced himself, was a handsome, dark-haired man in his early thirties. He showed my father a pass which identified him as an operative of SOE, Special Operations Executive, based on Baker Street — the organisation which Churchill said "would set Europe ablaze" — and he suggested a stroll around the damp and dark Portman Square.

"This must be quite a pleasant area to work in," said my father for the sake of something to say.

"I suspect it will be after the war," said Russell. "I really don't n-n-notice such things. I wanted to serve abroad, you see, but although I speak the lingo, I s-s-stammer in English."

My father would have smiled at that and thought of his own disabilities which had excluded him from a more active role, and felt an instant affinity with the man from SOE.

Russell lost no time in getting down to business. It was no secret, he said, that the allies would be invading northern Europe that year. What was essential was to fool the Germans as to when and, more importantly, where the landings would come. If the Germans thought the beachheads would be the Pas de Calais (the narrowest part of the Channel), then that's where the Panzer divisions would be stationed; totally useless if the invasion actually took place on, say, the Cherbourg peninsula, hundreds of miles away.

Where Sydney Seton, and the brewers, came in soon became clear.

As Russell rightly described, an invasion force required ships, landing craft, supplies of all sorts and men. Ships and supplies could be camouflaged or kept on the move, but men were more difficult. They had to be fed and watered during training, assembly and embarkation and they all required beer, even the Free French.

If you were invading at the Pas de Calais, explained Russell smoothly, then your invasion force would be based in East Anglia. If the target was the Cherbourg area, the marshalling zones would be Hampshire and Dorset or Devon. If you could find out where the invasion troops were massing, then you had a very good idea of where they would be landing. How did you discover where the troops were being billeted and trained? You followed the beer supplies.

The logic of it all would have been stunning to an innocent like my father. Most of the paperwork generated by the Beer For Troops committee was not even marked Confidential, let alone Secret. His own correspondence with Colonel Ayres, he realised, could have identified the location of two units of US Rangers on exercise in Scotland that month.

Something must be done about this, he would have said to Russell.

No, Russell, had replied, exactly the opposite.

Feed the *wrong* information about beer movements to the Germans, and on invasion day they will be in the wrong place looking in the wrong direction. Russell could do that, that was his job. But, of course, he needed the correct information to begin with — and very secretively, to make sure no one could suspect a trail of deliberate misinformation. Not even the Americans must know, or they might inadvertently break security.

For the following five months, my father doubled his trips to London, meeting Russell every fortnight and outlining the latest shipments and requirements of beer for troops, particularly the British forces in Southern Command and the massing Americans and Canadians. In fact, seeing my father off at Seagrave station was one of my earliest childhood memories, along with my mother saying he was "off to his war work".

Russell would meet my father either at the SOE or in Portman Square, using his regular visits to Colonel Ayres as "cover".

After several months of meetings, Russell expressed delight at the "intelligence" he was able to pass on. He openly hinted that my father's efforts would not go unrewarded.

It was in May 1944 that Russell, normally cool and business-like, became openly excited at their regular meeting.

My father had shown him the Brewers' Society circular of May 25th which advised all brewers that the Government and the Ministry of Food had revoked, with immediate effect, all export licences — which were required for sending beer to troops abroad. Furthermore, the Beer For Troops committee was authorised to advise members that the licences would be reinstated after "a short duration".

As if that was not enough to indicate that something big was afoot, the circular asked brewers to supply details of their current stock of export beer (i.e. bottled) and give an estimate of how much they could have ready by June 30th at the latest.

"This is it!" Russell had exclaimed. "Give me a t-t-tide table for France and I'll pinpoint the landings to the minute."

Less than two weeks later, on June 6th, the greatest armada in history appeared off the Normandy coast, heralded by airborne troops and backed by an air force of 11,000 planes, to begin the liberation of western Europe.

The Germans were caught napping, fully expecting the invasion to be in the Pas de Calais. In Seagrave, the church bells rang for the first time in nearly five years and closely guarded stocks of the brewery's barley wine were broken out and distributed to the workforce. My father, leading the celebrations, announced that — as soon as peace came — a new barley wine would be brewed in honour of our valiant forces fighting on the beaches in Normandy. Thus was "Gold Sword" promised, and my father was as good as his word. The name, he always said, chose itself. Gold and Sword were the two main British invasion beach code names. (Utah and Omaha were American, and Juno mostly Canadian.)

Gold Sword, which became a prize-winning beer, was seen by many brewer friends as a personal tribute to himself "for something Sydney did in the war", although my father never did breathe a word of his relationship with Harold Russell.

For his part, Russell also seemed to prove as good as his word.

My father was awarded the OBE in the first honours list published by the king after the war.

In fact, my father only saw Russell once after D-Day, and that was in 1949.

I was even introduced to him, as I was home from school for the summer vacation at the time. He had simply turned up at Seagrave station, amidst a crowd of holidaymakers, had telephoned the brewery and my father had sent a car for him. They lunched together in The Seton Arms hotel and Russell congratulated my father on his honour. He also asked if the Beer For Troops organisation, or rather its successor Export Committee, was involved in supplying Allied forces in West Germany. My father, who had cut down his visits to the Brewers' Society to rebuild the firm's peacetime trade, admitted that he did not know, as he was "a bit out of touch". Russell had said no matter, it wasn't important. Russell returned to London the same afternoon, staggering under the weight of a presentation crate of Gold Sword barley wine.

The brewery did well enough in the Fifties, and Gold Sword did extremely well, being listed by other brewers who had discontinued their own barley wines. The company remained firmly in family hands, my father owning the majority of shares, which would, in turn, come to me.

Even though I had gone up to Cambridge to read history, rather than Birmingham and the Brewing School, it was always expected that I would have "great expectations" in the firm — hence I became known as "Pip" rather than Philip.

It was a stunning blow, although my father told me before anyone else, when he announced that he was halting production of Gold Sword and approaching two large regional brewers with a view to selling the company. Later that year, it was 1963, he returned his OBE, and the following Spring, he retired to an isolated farmhouse ten miles inland from Seagrave where he remained a virtual recluse after the death of my mother in 1966, until his own, lonely death.

His retreat from business, brewing and all forms of public life (the Town Council, the Magistrates' Bench and so on) had been sparked by a chance turning on of the family television set in February 1963.

He rarely watched television, but a documentary caught his eye and he sat and followed it in total silence.

The programme was devoted to the story of a dark-haired, handsome man with a stammer who had disappeared from Beirut and was thought to be seeking asylum in the Soviet Union. It was claimed that he had held a senior position in British Intelligence while in fact he had been spying for Stalin since the 1930s.

His name was given as Harold Adrian Russell Philby.

Better known as Kim.

"No, I don't feel cheated of my heritage, Mr Potts," I said, keeping one eye on the road for my car and driver. "My father did what was best for the family — and himself — in the long run. And I've made a fair career for myself."

"You're one of these civil servant chappies, aren't you?" said Dr Crumley with a slight sneer.

"Yes. Foreign Office," I said vaguely, noticing with relief that Sergeant Evans was nosing the Jaguar round the corner of the church. Perhaps when I got back to the office I would have one last look at the file on Sydney Seton before it too was buried.

"Still can't understand about his OBE," said Potts. "He was proud of that. Odd thing to do — return it."

The Jaguar pulled up at the kerb and I said my goodbyes.

"It was because of the Beatles, Mr Potts," I lied. "That was all it was."